THE GREEN MAN

This book is a work of fiction. Names, characters, places, and incidents are the product of the author's imagination or are used fictitiously. Any resemblance to actual events, locales, corporate or government entities, facilities, or persons, living or dead, is coincidental.

A portion of this story first appeared in the *Ginosko Literary Journal.*

The Green Man

1st Edition

Story concept and text © 2025 by John Hughes

Cover design © 2025 Amidei Arte.

Editing, print preparation, formatting, back cover summary, and final cover design © 2025 Amidei Arte and © 2025 Staback Author Services.

Books may be ordered through popular, online retailers, Page Turner Books, Inc.'s online store, or by contacting the publisher at:

Page Turner Books, Inc.
222 N. Lafayette St., Suite 11
Shelby, NC 28150

Visit our website at www.ptbooksinc.com or contact us via email at contact@ptbooksinc.com. Page Turner Books, Inc.'s name and logo are copyright of Page Turner Books, Inc.

iBook ISBN: 978-1-965788-81-3
Kindle ISBN: 978-1-965788-82-0
Hardcover ISBN: 978-1-965788-83-7
Paperback ISBN: 978-1-965788-84-4

Library of Congress Control Number: 2025932659

Printed in the United States of America. First Printing: October 2025

THE GREEN MAN

JOHN CALVIN HUGHES

Shelby, NC, USA

Other Books by John Calvin Hughes

Cul-de-sac Agonistes

Killing Rush

Music From a Farther Room

The Boys

The Lost Gospel of Darnell Rabren

The Novels and Short Stories of Frederick Barthelme

The Shape of Our Luck

Twilight of the Lesser Gods

Voices Carry

PROLOGUE

Grand expanding universe, ancient beyond ancient. In the seconds after the Big Bang, nothing less than chaos was loosed. Before man was charged with good, there was evil. This swirly blue marble amid the blackness of space is the offspring of destruction, of colliding comets, splintering moons, and photons smashing on rock. Then came the glitter of receding galaxies. From the creation story to epic history, chronicles of sacred places, mountains, rivers, rocks, and groves abound. Yet hell is more than half of paradise. If there are sacred places, what of evil ones?

CHAPTER ONE

Within the tribe, there would be one....
~Mircea Eliade

Leah Grove stood before the red brick building, looking up at the windows of her new home: a two-bedroom unit in a gated condo community. She sighed. *You're moving backwards. This is like being in college again.* On the other hand, at least this place was not the wood and plaster apartment she'd lived in at Berkeley. It was roomy and well-built.

Still, a step down from living in a real house.

Living in New Haven with Timothy had been a sort of a dream. He was a lovely man, handsome, successful, and monied. He had wanted her, he had pursued her, and he had loved her. No doubt. But standing in a perfect house in a perfect neighborhood with a perfect man, she remembered a line of poetry—*in dreams begin responsibilities.* Just another beautiful phrase that didn't mean much to her until she plopped down in the middle of that perfect living room and tried to catch her breath.

She was torn, profoundly pulled in two directions. Maybe more. In the final analysis she had chosen her work, however badly she may have screwed that up, the work she felt was her destiny, over the dream of love. But, God, she missed him now. Especially his mouth, his lips and—

Enough. She straightened her shoulders and shook back the thick curls of her auburn hair and climbed the stairs. The slightly bent key gave her trouble, and the door was a little sticky, as if it hadn't been opened in a while, though she had looked at the apartment just last week with Mrs. Hendricks, the startlingly frail and elderly manager. She was a sweet, quiet woman in her sixties (or seventies, it was hard to say).

Leah had walked (slowly, oh so slowly) behind her up the narrow, concrete and metal steps, fully prepared to catch the old woman if she fell. Now Leah suffered a little moment of irrational panic, so she bumped her shoulder hard against the door, and it flew open.

The air in the apartment was musty. She propped the door open and raised all the windows and sat in the cool breeze, a wonderful surprise so early in September. *Mountain air,* she thought. *You live in the mountains.* Boxes of clothes and books crowded the small living room. She'd ordered a few things when she was still at her friend Elizabeth's in Connecticut. The coffee table, recliner and cheap bookshelves had arrived.

Mrs. Hendricks had kindly met the movers and let them in, probably taking charge and telling them where to put everything; and probably opened every box and rifled her possessions like a Cossack. Leah had accepted a temporary position at the University of Tennessee, Knoxville. She took the job for three reasons, really. One, she needed to put some distance between herself and the sensual pull of Timothy. Two, there were no other offers of employment; and three, she wanted to check out the Old Grey Cemetery.

She tiptoed through the boxes and suitcases and green bags, making plans as she went. *This here, that there. Just not right now.* Cool air drifted through the room. She felt sleepy, dreamy. Time to get moving. She looked around. The floor was one thing, but the walls! The empty walls! Intolerable. She went down to her car and began bringing up her art. *You might trip over boxes for a year, but you will look up from your falls and see beauty.*

Leah had decided some years ago that if she had extra money, she would spend it all on books and museum quality prints. Carefully, one by one, she toted her framed prints up the stairs and into the apartment. She lived by the popularly reviled notion that she might not know much about art, but she knew what she liked. No clichés for her. No starry nights, no fuzzy impressionist gardens, no existentialist screams, no melting clocks.

Against the biggest wall, she leaned Ed Mell's *Ascending Storm*. She wasn't sure where to put the others: Hokusai's *Bullfinch on Weeping Cherry*, Rousseau's *The Equatorial Jungle*, plus the others still in the car. But she needed to hang the Mell now. She went to the kitchen to scavenge the boxes for a hammer and nail. She hung it, and stood before the print, and felt better.

She spent the next half hour hauling up the house plants she'd refused to leave at Timothy's. He'd have let them die. Not out of spite or even indifference. She didn't think he'd ever even noticed them.

She'd been forced to leave Yale because she had messed up. Royally. She took grant money to do research and had promised the grant committee a certain kind of research—but she had done something else entirely. "Wasted money and effort" was what the letter from the committee had read, and her contract had not been renewed. So much for the Ivy League. *When Tennessee finds out about you, you'll surely be out on your butt and wind up at some community college!*

She had written her dissertation at Yale. It was a study of sacred places. Her committee had loved it. She had been offered a position as a junior professor which she accepted, and almost immediately she had been awarded a grant with a bunch of money so that she could go visit some of the major sacred spots like Machu Picchu, Stonehenge, Meteora, and the Three Holy Mountains. The idea was to expand her dissertation into what her advisors assured her would be a ground-breaking book on the subject.

A year later she stood in the middle of Timothy's perfect house, asking herself why she was leaving. Leah found herself beyond language, unable to explain why this place, this perfect place, was utterly and unforgivably wrong for her right now. *Timing is everything and Time has screwed you over.*

So she left him. Left him there in New Haven with his family's money and that beautiful house and left the college and the leaves turning ever so slightly in the wind, falling around her in a blazing death of reds and golds. She had picked up the dead leaves and woven them into her blouse and her hair. Now, standing at the window of her new home, she remembered the dusty odor of those leaves.

There was something else too—something old and eerie reaching down in the wind from the mountains, smoky and blue at the edge of the world.

* * * * *

A light rain blew against the north side of the building, so she closed that window and set about unpacking the small groceries she had bought. The Mell print was hung; but the others would have to wait. Leah had bought a piece of salmon, and now she stared at it, wondering how badly she was going to stink up the place trying to blacken it. She had pooh-poohed the butcher's ready-made blackening mix in favor of concocting her own. She lined up the spices: paprika, cayenne pepper, onion powder, salt, white pepper, black pepper, thyme, basil and oregano.

She looked doubtfully at her cast-iron cornbread skillet. In truth, it seemed to be giving her a look. Like it was saying in her Grandmother Effie's voice, "*Don't fry fish in me, darling. I'm for cornbread.*" Now the fish was coated and the pan smoking. She dropped the filet into the pan where it sizzled pleasantly. She turned it once. It stuck a little, and a little more when she took it out. Wracked with guilt, she washed the skillet with hot water and sea salt and dried it completely with her best towel. When she was done and the pan safely in the cabinet, the fish was a little cold but tasted great. She looked at her empty plate. Probably should have made a salad or some green beans or something to go with it. *Does Effie still cook? She would have done better than you.*

Leah took her coffee on the little balcony. She shook the folding chair open—only a little damp—propped her feet on the railing and looked around. Everything was clean and wet, surfaces sparkling, the air clear. The sun was full on some places, while others were still in shadow, the sky broken with dark clouds and patches of brilliant blue. She hadn't really looked around the place yet. She was not even sure where the swimming pool was, not that it would matter, what with autumn on the way.

The Greymont wasn't a large complex. Nine buildings like bean rows in a crazy garden, dropped randomly through the narrow and long property. Her balcony didn't face another building, rather the back wall of the complex which separated the beautiful, lush spread of St. Augustine lawn from a stand of trees out beyond the wall—or woods might be a better description. What she could see of the wall was stone and mortar, mostly obscured by vines and plants climbing over from the other side.

Something was drawing her eye to the trees beyond the wall, something not quite—what? A glow? A chilling breeze? No. A smell, a stink. The disconcerting odor of the overripe, of the feculent, something muddy, something sour. Then she saw the girl.

The sky was tumbling toward indigo. A thin line of crimson outlined the mountains in the distance. Dusk crawled along the surface of the earth, inching its way toward the apartment complex. No one was in sight. Except for the girl.

She was probably eight or nine years old. She wore a red shift with tiny white polka-dots and stood perfectly still. Leah put her full attention on the child who stood no more than a foot or two from the wall, seemingly just staring at it, not moving.

After what seemed like a long time, but might have been only a minute, the girl still hadn't moved.

Leah stood up and leaned on the railing. She was trying to see the girl's face. From that angle, Leah could barely make out the child's eyes. Were they open? *What is this kid doing?* The child seemed to be saying something, her lips barely moving. At that distance Leah couldn't hear her.

Now Leah noticed that the girl seemed to be standing in a little pile of vines. One of her shoes was completely covered, and strangely, the vines seemed woven around her foot as if she'd stepped into a nest of some kind. One of the tendrils was sticking up at such an angle as to appear to be trailing up the child's leg. Like, maybe, she'd been standing there for days, and the vine was using her as a pole, a dowel or whatever, and now the other shoe was covered too—*hadn't Leah just seen it?*—and she opened her mouth to call out to the child but stopped.

What did she think she would say? She couldn't even call the child's name. She didn't know it. *What, just yell out, 'Hey you!' to some kid you don't know and you being the new person in the place—the unknown, the stranger? No way. Can't be done.*

Then, without turning, the girl raised her arm and pointed back toward the building, toward Leah on her balcony.

Toward me? Why? What is going on?

Leah leaned forward to get a better view, but she got woozy, and the ground below seemed to spin. She sat down hard on the floor and leaned her head against the bars of the railing. The dizziness overwhelmed her so much she thought she might throw up. When she looked out again toward the girl, she was gone.

Or—wait. *Is that a bit of cloth, red and white, against the vines on the wall?*

The vines seemed to shiver, and the cloth was gone, as if it had been sucked into the wall.

Not possible, she thought.

Her legs felt rubbery. She didn't feel secure on the balcony, this close to the railing, so she didn't try to stand, rather scooted on her bum until her back was against the sliding glass door. She reached up and pulled the door open and fell backwards into the small bedroom. She lay on the floor, trying to catch her breath and willing the ceiling to stop spinning—she couldn't get a really good deep breath—.

She crawled into the kitchen and pulled herself up to the sink. She let cold water run over her wrists. She splashed some on her face, then she stumbled through the apartment and out the door. Leah walked down the dangerous metal and brutal concrete steps and around the side of the building toward the back wall.

Nothing.

A hawk cried somewhere out in the woods. The child was gone. No sign of her.

What the hell is going on? She lurched up and down the yard along the wall. *Don't freak out now.* She didn't see the girl anywhere. *It's okay. The kid just went home.*

The hawk cried again, this time closer. Fat squirrels ran up and down the thin oaks. Sometimes they ran out into the lawn toward the wall, then ran quickly back where they'd come from—up into the oaks, where they swayed on slender branches.

And just then, a voice called, "Rachel! Rachel, come here," from somewhere back toward the front of the building. A woman stepped into view and called Rachel once more. She looked at Leah a long second, then turned away. The hawk cried again. No answer.

Back in her apartment, she took to the recliner and sat bolt upright with her hands gripping the armrests as if she were on an airplane taking off during a thunderstorm. As if to reinforce this image into her head, thunder rumbled off in the distance. She reclined the chair and fell into an uneasy sleep.

All night the ancient stars wheeled overhead, throwing their light into the dark places in the woods beyond the wall. She had dream after dream of being lost, unable to find her car, her house, her classroom, wandering helplessly as familiar landscapes became more and more unrecognizable, mute before the dream inhabitants who might help her find her way, if she could just find her voice.

* * * * *

Someone was knocking on her door.

Leah stumbled out of the chair, stiff and achy from sleeping there all night. She coughed and then recoiled from the miasma that was her own morning breath. *Did something die in my guts?* She glanced at the kitchen trying to decide whether to make coffee or open the door.

She heard the knocking again, a little more insistent this time. She looked through the peephole and saw the apartment manager, Mrs. Hendricks. Leah leaned her head against the door and sighed. She mustered up the best smile she could and opened the door.

Mrs. Hendricks was wearing some kind of gardening outfit, khaki pants, denim shirt, floppy hat, and gesturing at Leah with a trowel.

"Sweetie," she drawled, "you need to turn in that paperwork I gave you. You rented this place two weeks ago. So much depends—"

"I'm sorry, I've been so busy, trying, you know, to get everything squared away, here and at work. I just got here yesterday, you know."

Mrs. Hendricks looked around the living room at the unpacked boxes, piles of books and unhung up clothes and clicked her tongue.

"Yes, it is difficult getting settled in. Decisions just seem to take on momentous import, don't they?"

She picked up the forms from the littered coffee table.

"I'll leave you to it, but do try to get this done, dearie," and she turned toward the door.

"Wait! Mrs. Hendricks. I, uh, I saw a little girl last night. Out by the back wall. Do you know who she is?"

"Goodness. Last night? It was very dark last night. Where did you say she was?"

"Well, no, it wasn't full night. It was almost dark, dusk, you know. Twilight. She was standing out by the wall. It was, I don't know, kind of weird."

"In what way weird, dear?"

Leah could hear what she would sound like to Mrs. Hendricks: the girl looked like she was talking to the wall, the girl acted like the wall was talking to her, the vines seemed to be grabbing—uh, well. And she had pointed at Leah.

She could see the girl now in her mind, her arm reaching back to point up toward Leah, and the dizzy feeling that came over her. She felt it now.

"Are you all right, dear?" Mrs. Hendricks was helping her into the recliner. "You're white as a sheet."

Mrs. Hendricks found a clean dish towel, soaked and wrung it out, and laid it on Leah's forehead.

"Just sit here. Lean that chair back and rest a minute."

Leah closed her eyes and listened to Mrs. Hendricks rattling things in the kitchen. After a minute, Mrs. Hendricks said she needed something from her apartment, and that she would return in a moment. Leah might have slept (or passed out) for a moment because the next thing she knew, Mrs. Hendricks was back in her kitchen rattling things again.

Leah pulled the towel down and rubbed her eyes with it. When she looked up, Mrs. Hendricks was placing a tray on the coffee table. The tray held a plastic bottle of Perrier, five Oreos, and what might have been a child's toy tea service, except that the pot was clearly steaming.

"Miss Grove, I'm not a doctor, of course, but I think you might be a little dehydrated, maybe even a little low on your blood sugar. When's the last time you ate?"

Leah opened her mouth.

Mrs. Hendricks waved a dismissive hand.

"Never mind. I want you to drink half of this bottle of water right now."

She twisted the top off and handed the bottle to Leah. Mrs. Hendricks nodded at the bottle, and Leah drank.

She was thirsty, for she drank half the bottle quickly, enjoying the slightly burning quality of sparkling water. She might have finished it had Mrs. Hendricks not taken it from her.

Mrs. Hendricks poured a cup of tea and said, "It's Morning Thunder. Milk?"

Leah raised an eyebrow.

"It's all I had, dear. Eat a cookie now, it'll be good for you."

Leah did as she was told while Mrs. Hendricks chattered about the goings on of the apartment complex. No gossip she, Mrs. Hendricks' remarks were limited to a vigorous jeremiad on the host of Sisyphean tasks involved in running a place like The Greymont: the recalcitrant tenants, their petty concerns and bickering, the lazy groundskeepers…Oh it was enough to put one into an early grave, don't you know.

"The girl," Leah said. "Do you know—"

"What girl? Oh, you mean the little girl out after dark? I'm not sure who that would be. What did she look like?"

When Leah had described her, Mrs. Hendricks said, "Could be somebody's granddaughter. We don't have anyone that age living here now. You might have noticed, The Greymont is aptly named. It's practically a retirement home. You won't find your Adam's rib here, sweetie. The youngest man in this place is a hundred. Even at my age, I don't want any of them," and she giggled.

"Wouldn't an Adam's rib be a woman?" Leah said.

Mrs. Hendricks smiled.

"Oh, I don't judge, sweetie."

Leah drank two cups of tea and ate all the Oreos.

Mrs. Hendricks left, and Leah took a shower. She spent the day organizing her clothes and getting some of her books onto the cheap big box store bookshelves she screwed together one at a time as she filled them. She reminded herself to drink water all day and had a thick pb&j and lots of chips for lunch. By six-thirty, the clothes were pretty much done, and she'd filled the last bookshelf, although she had not yet emptied the last three boxes of books. She'd order more shelves tomorrow.

* * * * *

In the back of Leah's mind as she worked was Timothy. She tried to think of other things, but her tasks were so simple that he was always there. Every little lapse in her thoughts now crowded with visions of him. She kept remembering him taking off his shirt. It was the first thing he did coming in the door every evening. Then he would stand there, naked from the waist up, looking the shirt over for imperfections, any excuse to throw it out and buy a new one, the muscles in his back rippling like windblown silk. The sight of him stretching out the kinks of the day invariably made her wet. And she would step out of her pants and kick them across the floor at him. And he would unzip his trousers and—*Stop now. You need to stop right now.*

She had met Timothy in New Haven. Being accepted into the doctoral program at Yale astonished her, though her advisor and teachers at Berkeley evinced no surprise at all. She had found the town much to her liking.

Like Berkeley, New Haven was small enough for Leah to feel a part of. Its changes of elevation were even more delightful than Berkeley's. Her favorite thing about both her cities was that she could find a high venue from which to look out over the whole town, to have it spread before her and yet, somehow, within her grasp.

New Haven was dominated by two great trap rock ridges, what the locals called East Rock and West Rock. Both were homes to rambling parks where she could wander for hours and think about the sacred places of the world which she had dedicated her life and her energies to studying. The more she studied, the more she wrote, the more she walked among the trees and rocks above New Haven, the more she felt the numinous glow of the divine in the natural world. She had found a sub-let in Oyster Point near the water. The campus was a little too far for her to walk, so she bicycled until it got too cold. After that she took the bus.

It took her a while to adjust to the cold of Connecticut. True, a summer in Berkeley was the coldest winter she ever spent, but on the upside, it never snowed.

She had grown up in Oklahoma and lived there for the first eighteen years of her life. Flat as a flit, as her father said so many times.

Tom Grove must have said a million things to her. Why did she remember only that with any clarity? When she thought of him, when she pictured him, tall, rangy, windburnt, he was facing the lowering sun, that long slanting light, almost horizontal, firing across the flat landscape, casting every object, every person into golden relief. He was a distant man who found no solace in conversation.

Her mother, Connie, Connie Grove nee Rabren, was not much better. She hadn't wanted children and had been talked out of terminating Leah by some church ladies, according to her grandmother. Connie was also reticent. Whatever task was at hand, she always seemed to be looking at something a million miles away, out there where the sky meets the earth, where, Leah supposed, her dreams had gone to die.

Tom Grove had come to Oklahoma to improve the wheat. He loved plants. Hed had gone to the University of Texas at Austin to study religion and become a preacher. Wanting to avoid the terrible things he imagined in the biology labs, he took botany, just to get one of his science courses out of the way. He fell in love with it and changed his major.

His mother, who'd dreamed of him in the pulpit had died in his freshman year. She had been beyond complaint. His father didn't care one way or the other. Tom always had a garden. Leah's earliest memories were of sitting on the ground by his vegetable garden while he worked. He gardened, she realized later, with the care and gentleness of the besotted amateur. He hoed around corn stalks with a precision and devotion comparable to love. He told her he would have nine beans rows. And a beehive. She remembered that. The reference to Yeats. In reality, he had thirteen bean rows and no hive at all.

Talkative, outgoing, and curious, Leah wondered a thousand times if she were a changeling. Had fairies stolen the real Leah and left her in Connie and Tom's care? She had her father's eyes and her mother's hands. Still, who knew what fairies are capable of.

Come away, O human child! To the waters and the wild with a faery, hand in hand. For the world's more full of weeping than you can understand.

Was the real Leah somewhere out there, by the fairy waters, in the salley gardens, at the brown river god's crumbling edge, dancing in a pixie ring and leaving poor changeling Leah in an Oklahoma flattened by the mad hand of God, her parents gone, from her and the world.

Well, whichever Leah she was, when her parents died, they left her nothing but their intelligence. She had made her way to Berkeley and was admitted on the strength of her SAT scores, despite the high school equivalency certificate she'd gotten a week before applying. Aced every course, every science, every language, every art, music, and literature they could throw at her. Leah worked every night at a burger joint, until she was given a full scholarship to finish her degree. Then she went straight into a master's program on a full ride. No one but she was surprised when she was accepted at Yale to work toward her Ph.D.

Yale was her first foray into teaching. As part of her fellowship, she was required to teach two classes to undergraduates in the Religion Department. She felt ridiculous standing in front of these Yale freshmen, lecturing them on the history of religion. Their faces suggested they knew more than she did on the subject. For that matter, she looked younger than most of them. She certainly felt younger. Yet they treated her with respect, turned in their brilliant papers, and got their A's. At least it was easy work, talking about things that interested her, and not a soul-crushing gig flipping burgers or schlepping drinks at some fern bar.

One night at the Gryphon, Tommy, the much-too-cute waiter whose section she always sat in, came over with a dirty martini. They looked at each other: it was a game they played. Tommy knew she was going to send the drink back to whatever man had sent it, so he would never actually set the drink before her. He held it at eye level for her. She would look at the drink, then look at Tommy (both would raise their eyebrows), then they would turn to face the offending drink-buyer.

Leah didn't accept drinks. She wasn't interested in some bar guy or in dating. No, Leah was focused. She was going to get her degree. Leah was going to get a grant and change the world. She has a perfectly serviceable vibrator in her nightstand.

When she saw the young man in the Brioni pinstripes, looking at her over his own dirty martini, eyes as blue as arctic ice, she took the drink from Tommy and set it primly in front of her. And she smiled.

Tommy nodded admiringly toward the man and headed back to the bar. She'd never once accepted a drink. But tonight? *Well*, Leah thought, *he is as hot as hinges.*

"I'm Timothy Lowell," he said as he sat down across from her. "I'm going to guess you're studying for your, oh let's say, Masters, in, hm, Literature."

Leah raised one eyebrow. The left.

She'd spent hours as a teenager in front of the mirror working her eyebrows. One of the ladies who'd worked in the orphanage had complete control over her brows. She could send one or the other up, shooting the left one up like a rocket when Leah's lie was outrageously transparent or the right one ever so slightly to indicate a whisper of a doubt. Leah could raise them both when she first tried. Hours, hours, and then the left one moved ever so slightly without its twin, and eventually she could make them bounce like caterpillars on crack.

"And, let's see, not the Romantics. No, none of that beauty and sentience of nature stuff for you. No, you're a Modernist. T.S. Eliot and Pound. Hemingway. No, wait. That's ridiculous. All that misogynistic formalism. You're studying women. Woolf, Kate Chopin, uh—"

"Let me stop you right there. You took a wrong turn at Literature. I'm not studying literature."

Timothy blushed.

"Does this little game usually work?"

"I—uh...."

"I mean, are you really that good a profiler. A pick-up artist profiler. Let me guess, you were about to quote me some poetry. Something you have memorized given the period of literature you think I study."

"I don't have any poetry memorized."

"And yet you should. You should have some memorized. Oh, let's say, *Though nothing can bring back the hour of splendor in the grass, of glory in the flower, we will grieve not, rather find strength in what remains behind.* No. Wait. Maybe something more romantic. More of a *Shall I compare thee to a summer's day. Thou art more lovely and more temperate,* kind of thing, huh?"

Timothy blushed.

"But you're not a literature student—"

Leah cut him off.

"And what if you were profiling some med student? I'm guessing you'd know her area of study because she would stink of formaldehyde. That's a real giveaway. The smell of death and rotten meat from the breath of your potential mistress reeks? Do you then have some medical trivia at the ready?"

"I know there are 24 bones in the human hand," Timothy said, trying to catch up.

"That's the squirrel hand. There are 27 in the human hand."

"Okay," Timothy ducked his head. "Fine. You're smart, really smart. But surely you're not as mean as you're pretending to be."

"So, do you ever guess correctly? The field of study of your victims?"

"My victims! Hold on, hold on. I tried to guess your major. How's that a crime?"

"Do you ever guess right?"

"Actually—this is the first time I tried that."

"Mm hm. I'm sure."

Timothy had fumbled around in that cute way he had and finally gotten a smile out of Leah. *Oh god, his mouth!* He bought her dinner that night, but she wouldn't agree to see him again for a week, even though he called and asked her out every night. He was too good looking. There had to be something wrong with him, something badly wrong. His lips, though. *Oh my god his lips are a pornographic poem!*

She pictured those lips every night, burning out the batteries in her vibrator.

Friday three weeks on, she did finally agree to a second date. Saturday. He told her they were going to eat over in Morris.

Morris! Who goes to Morris to eat, she'd wondered.

She Googled the restaurant he named, the Schloss. If there were a more expensive one in Connecticut, she couldn't find it. Their wine list seemed to take up the whole internet. And so, what the heck, she Googled him too.

Surprise, surprise! He was rich. She told him to pick her up at the school. She didn't want him to know where she lived, at least not yet.

He arrived in a Cadillac XTS. Navy, with burgundy interior.

When Timothy opened the passenger door for her, she said, "I'm riding up front with the chauffeur? Really?"

"What chauffeur? I'm driving."

He sounded a little exasperated.

Leah shrugged and got in. She could see him talking to himself as he walked around the front.

When he got in, he shut the door a little harder than he had to. He cranked the car and pulled out into traffic.

So—he's sensitive on the issue of money. Fine.

"How far to this place?" she said.

"Less than an hour."

He didn't elaborate. He was pouting, she thought. He didn't say anything else.

She, on the other hand, felt no need to force or carry the conversation. The ball was in his court. *Remember, he asked you out, not the other way around.* He needed to impress her, not the other way around. They listened to some opera all the way. Wagner, maybe? Boring.

Leah suspected they were given the best table in the place, but, after looking around, she really didn't see any tables that weren't excellent. The walls were glass and reflected the dining room back at her.

A man in a white tuxedo (and lipstick and foundation, maybe, it was hard to tell) played a white baby grand piano in the corner.

Without looking at the menu, Timothy said he was ordering the duck breast and beet salad.

She asked him what was good.

This seemed to finally bring him out of his mood, and he talked excitedly about the different choices on the menu. He seemed genuinely pleased by her selection of the Seared Stonington scallops. He ordered a chardonnay she had noticed on the menu at one hundred twenty-five dollars a bottle. But she didn't say anything. The food was good. Really good.

For dessert, banana bread tiramisu in edible chocolate shells. She did everything in her power not to show how absolutely, world-destroyingly delicious it was.

In truth, she just tried not to fall face first into it.

On the ride home, the car was warm, and she was full. Drowsy. Trees close to the road flew past, lit out of the blackness by the car's headlights. She could see the lights of New Haven bleeding up into the sky, turning it dark violet, starless and hazy.

Timothy had chosen a classical music station, probably WSHU, and a Vivaldi concerto filled the car with long strings in a minor key.

She may have fallen asleep, for she startled when he stopped before her apartment building. She ran the back of her hand across her mouth. At least she hadn't been drooling.

He sat looking ahead with his hands still on the wheel.

She looked at his profile. *God, he was handsome.* The lights of passing cars lit the planes of his face and she understood how boys could so easily mistake lust for love. She might well be in lust this very moment. She roused herself and reached for the door handle. Quickly he was out of the car and holding the door open for her, extending a hand. So gallant.

"You are not coming in," she said.

"Did I ask to come in?"

"I'm just saying."

He snorted.

"'I'm just saying.' Of all the empty things people say to one another these days, I think I find that the most insipid."

"'Insipid'?"

"Think about it," he said and leaned in and kissed her cheek, then got in his, what…eighty-thousand-dollar car and drove away, leaving her on the sidewalk, sputtering.

Did he just call you insipid? She lay awake half the night considering the implications of "I'm just saying."

He was right. On the other hand, admitting it to herself didn't help her fall asleep.

Wait. How did he know where you live? Damn, I bet he Googled you too. Or does he have a private detective on retainer?

* * * * *

The end of her second day at the Greymont she considered ordering pizza. Or some Chinese. The night sky was murky, the stars watery, and the horn of the moon about to slide down into the woods. In the western sky, she could see Mars, throbbing red in the misty sky, unusually bright, oddly so. She passed the lush St. Augustine yard that stretched away toward the back wall, the grass cool against her snow-white feet.

What was that faint glow beyond the wall, somewhere out in the woods? An optical illusion of some kind...a hallucination? Where had the little girl been standing? A lone dead tree reached up from somewhere out in the middle of the grove. It seemed underlit by something glowing greenly from below.

She shook her head. The place was getting to her. Too quiet. Deadly silent, she thought. Not a cricket, nor cicada. Not a lonely dog barking anywhere. Where was everybody? She hadn't seen one neighbor yet. She walked toward the back wall.

It was darker so far back here, under the overhanging trees. She could barely see the wall. She knew it was covered with vines that had grown over from the other side. Had the groundskeepers allowed this? Did they imagine the growth to be attractive, rustic, and charming in some way? She peered at the vines on the wall, trying to see them more clearly. She squeezed her eyes shut tightly to improve her night vision, but when she opened them, the world was even darker than before, if anything. In the depths of the tangled vines she noticed a faint red patch, roundish, like a rose or a spot of blood. Could a wild rose have climbed the wall and be blooming in September?

She inched closer to the wall.

Leaves on low-hanging limbs brushed against her hair and a strand of spider web touched and stuck to her cheek. She shuddered. It was chilly here close to the wall, as if the stones were cold and radiating cold and making her cold too. She squinted, trying to get the red splotch into focus. Blurry, it seemed to be undulating, roiling like something alive, giving off little wisps of color that evaporated into the surrounding darkness. She put out her hand.

For a moment, everything stopped. Not a leaf moved, not a breath of wind. But more so, the silence deepened, as if she were in the place between songs on a CD. A soul-wrenching quiet. And in the quiet she watched her hand, fuzzy white against the black of the night, creep between the vines toward the rose, for a rose she had decided it was, and though it looked just within her reach, she could not grasp it. She pushed her arm farther in, until her shoulder was flush against the knotty tangle of vines. It occurred to her that she should be touching the wall by now, that she was reaching far enough for her hand to be on the other side of the wall. Had she found an aperture, some opening through—

Ouch!

She yanked her hand back. Something had pricked her thumb. She backed away and looked at her hand.

A drop of blood, black in the fuzzy starlight, stood on the tip of her throbbing thumb. She stuck her thumb into her mouth, and under the familiar salty iron tang of her own blood, familiar as an old radio song, she tasted—what? A color? A mood? A poison?

She spat and headed back toward the lights of the parking area beyond her building. Now she could feel dew on the grass. Was it that late? Or early? She felt chilled to the bone and her thumb throbbed. She almost put it in her mouth again but thought better of it. She turned the corner of the structure and made her way to the stairs. Her feet felt numb against the cold concrete steps, as if she were wearing slippers. She could feel the stairs and yet not feel them. She fumbled the key into the lock and let herself inside.

Her apartment still held the warmth of the day. She shivered in gratitude and went into the bathroom, where she turned on the shower as hot as it would go and sat in the back of the tub with her legs pulled up against her, just out of reach of the scalding spray. She luxuriated in the steam as her thumb pulsed. She squeezed it and a drop of blood oozed up. It looked too dark like when an artist adds black to his paint to produce a shade of the color she wants. She put her thumb under the spray and watched the blood wash over her hand and away down the drain.

That night Leah dreamed about being lost again, one of those school dreams. She was supposed to teach a class, but she was late and couldn't find the classroom. Every corner she turned, every hallway she ran down, the place became more unfamiliar. Shortcuts she thought she knew led her farther and farther from anything she recognized. Strange buildings loomed, their loading docks weirdly familiar. A lake in the middle of campus. No one in sight. No help to be expected. The horizon pulsing yellow, red, yellow, red. She woke up breathing hard and panicky, heart pounding.

It's just that you're starting a new job now. You don't know the campus. You're disoriented. You're in a new place. You'll find your way, quit worrying. Classes don't start for another week. You can go over early, find the rooms you teach in, find your office if they assign you one. But everything will be okay. Everything will be fine.

But she couldn't shake the feeling even after three cups of the full pot of coffee she made the next morning. It was more than just dislocation, she knew. It was this quest she'd taken on, this path that had called her and ruinated her life and her career.

And who exactly do you think you are anyway? Gawain? Ahab?

She spent the day emptying boxes and filling drawers and closets, hanging pictures, watering plants—*my goodness, they're thriving! And after all that time riding in the trunk of her car.* The work was mindless, comforting. Every once in a while, she put her hand on something that reminded her of Timothy. As if she needed reminding. As if he weren't in her head every minute. Timing is everything. He was a wonderful man, and maybe, just maybe, he had been exactly right for her. Like the third chair, the third porridge bowl, the third bed, but the timing was wrong. Yes, he was ungodly gorgeous, smart, and funny. Hell, she could admit it...he was a blazing hot advertisement for heterosexuality. But timing. Timing is everything.

Back in New Haven, Leah had found it hard to keep Timothy at bay. Though she would only agree to see him one night a week, Friday or Saturday depending on her study schedule, he called her and sent flowers during the week. Though she didn't take his calls until the weekend, she did enjoy the flowers on her desk and by her bed. Yes, she knew that behind their color and bouquet was the thought of Timothy. Which just what he wanted—to be there, in her house, in her mind, floating like the fragrance of roses or gardenias from room to room.

But she had other fish to fry, so to speak. His life—the money, the prestige, the social obligations—no, she was going somewhere else in life, and she was going to be something, and she was not going to become the bejeweled arm candy of some Richie Rich, no matter how gorgeous, how funny, how rich, how kind. No matter what her heart kept telling her about him. She hadn't worked like a field hand, beaten the odds, survived this long to spend her life arranging petit fours on silver trays or stirring martinis for his rich friends and rich family.

And the sex! Well, damn.

Eventually, she had allowed him into her bed. His body was Greek god gorgeous, and he knew how to use it.

Leah had not let him in her apartment. Yet. Some part of that was embarrassment. The place was shabby and filled with homemade bookcases. She had bought her sad little bed at Goodwill. Her sheets were clean but stained. She had her nice prints on the wall, but they couldn't disguise the fact that she was a dirt-broke grad student with a pantry full of boil-in-bag noodles and Campbell's soup.

It was a Friday night at the end of the semester. She was done with all the work for her classes and only had meetings with professors the following week. He had taken her to a cheap family restaurant for dinner, and they had taken a stroll along Church Street and stopped to admire the old Gothic City Hall building. She had let him kiss her hard and long right there in front of God and everybody.

When he drove her home and walked her to the door, she said, "I have a bottle of wine that I think you might enjoy if you want to come in for a while."

His mouth, his beautiful mouth, hung open for a second and then he enthusiastically agreed that, yes, wine would be good. Yes, he'd love to come in. Thank you, that'd be great.

They never opened the wine.

As soon as the door was shut, she threw herself against him and kissed him for all she was worth. She had him pushed back against the door, and he put his hands on her breasts, rubbing them and feeling for the nipples which he squeezed gently. They stood up under his fingers and he fumbled with the buttons of her blouse, trying to get under the cloth to the naked skin. She slid her hand down the front of his pants and grabbed his cock. The look on his face was priceless.

They pulled at each other's clothes in a frenzy, kissing and undressing at the same time, falling over their pants, finally breaking away from each other in order to get completely naked and then meeting in the middle of the mattress.

To feel the length of his body against her!

That night they broke her poor bed, and he bought her a new one the next day. After that, they slept at his place.

Money. Money everywhere.

And he was beautiful. And smart. And decent. So, after a couple of weeks, she just straight up moved in with him.

God, the money! There was never a question about it. Can we afford this? She stopped asking. His house in Prospect Hill was not only the nicest place she'd ever lived, but was, in fact, the nicest place she'd ever been in! Soon it was full of his friends and colleagues, her few acquaintances among the student body. Soon her life became his.

Night after night, she climaxed, on his fingers, on his tongue, on his cock. His sculptured body! Then, one night, it was a Tuesday, she remembered it well: she lay next to him, spent and sweaty and satisfied. Again. And that's when she freaked.

She could see the life she had worked so hard for coming to a glorious, twilight-of-the-gods end. Trading her hard work, her long hours, her desperate scholarship, her survival against fire and death for sweet satisfying sex and sleep on soft Egyptian cotton and cold vodka drinks in Baccarat lead crystal and quiet air conditioning.

She could feel everything slipping away from her. Had it been her idea to move in with him or his? She couldn't remember. But moving in was a mistake. She should have kept him further removed. What kind of bullshit ethos demanded she play house with a man just because she liked to have sex with him? Okay, she liked him too. Enjoyed his company. Yes, all of that. But move in. It had certainly seemed like the thing to do.

She was teaching an Introduction to the Gospels class. It consisted of serious, buttoned-down young men and frilly-collared young women all headed toward work in the ministry. They were serious, studious and pious. All except one.

His name was Quentin Bon.

At the first class meeting everyone introduced themselves, starting with Leah. After everyone else had told their short bios, Leah had to prompt the young man to his feet.

Young man indeed. She was probably no more than three years his senior. He said that he was studying poetry and intended to take up the mantle of poetry himself. He'd then spend the rest of his life paying off his Yale education turning over hamburgers in the greasiest spoon he could find.

She laughed.

He was a good student, but of course he had no Greek or Latin. Since it was a freshman intro course, languages weren't required. Exactly. He dressed in blacks and grays, never combed his thick black curls, and had dirt under his fingernails. She could smell his dirty clothes from the back of the room.

She used him. No matter how she might rationalize herself, she seduced her student and slept with him as a way out of her future with Timothy. His little apartment was worse than hers had been. His roommates sat on a broken-down couch watching television and drinking beer while they fucked on a mattress on the floor in the one bedroom beyond the paper-thin wall.

When they were finished, she lay panting beside him, suddenly aware of how squalid the place really was.

The cleaning lady changed the sheets on Timothy's bed (*our bed, our bed!*) twice a week. They literally still smelled clean when she pulled them off and replaced them.

Quentin's sheets, if this was in fact his bed, were surely second hand and had probably never been laundered since they were stretched over this saggy mattress the first time. The pillows smelled sour, and the corners of the tiny room were moldy.

Don't ask yourself what you're doing here. You know exactly what you're doing.

Quentin lit a cigarette and read her a couple of his poems while ashes fell on his chest. The words bounced around the room and didn't really make any sense. Not to say they were bad. Who knows? She always had to read poetry on the page to make any sense of it. Poetry readings went over her head.

"So, rumor has it that John Ashbury is giving a reading in whatever Hall next week."

Leah sighed.

"Maybe we could go together."

"Think about that for a minute, Quentin."

"Well, nobody would have to know we were together together. We could just act like it was a coincidence. Don't you think?"

"That's not how rumor works. Let's say we did meet by accident at the reading. And that we sat together to hear the great poet speak. And that we were not sleeping together. Rumor would put us together anyway. See?"

"You just don't want to go."

"Well, there's that. But more to the point, I'd like to hold on to my job. And my reputation."

"Gotcha. Well, okay. So, can we fuck again?"

She rolled on top of him and said, "That's what we're here for."

She continued to meet Quentin a couple of times a week. Mostly in the afternoon, after her classes and before Timothy got home from work. Always in his atrocious little place. She'd scrub herself mercilessly in the shower before Timothy's arrival. She didn't do it so much to get Quentin off of her, but she thought she could smell his place on her, in her hair, and on her clothes.

One day while he was at work, she called a moving company and had the men empty the back bedroom where Timothy had put all her things from her apartment in Oyster Point. Maybe he thought she would eventually just sell it all on eBay or gift it to some charity. Her paintings were stacked facing the wall, her plants pale and etiolated, stretching toward the north-facing window.

After the men had loaded the truck, she sent them to a storage unit she'd rented over the phone while they worked. She then loaded her car. She took a last look around. She and Timothy hadn't had flatware. They had silverware. Real silver silverware. When they ate the canned soups she liked, they used spoons that cost more than a hundred cans of soup.

Now she took one and bent it and left it in the middle of the dining room table. She wasn't going to write a note. Let him read what he would into the bent spoon.

She hauled her clothes and books and plants down to her car. She drove to Elizabeth's house out from the city.

Elizabeth was the only real friend she'd made in New Haven. They'd met in the framing shop where Liz worked downtown. Liz had been intrigued by the Mell poster Leah was having framed and they talked about Mell and some other artists they liked. They ended up having lunch and becoming friends. Now she and Elizabeth carried the plants onto the wide front porch and Liz yanked a water hose up and soaked them to the very roots.

"Thanks for doing this."

"What? Watering your plants? Hiding your car from your ex? What are friends for?"

"Not hiding it, just—okay, fine, hiding it."

"And what now?"

"Carry me to the airport tomorrow."

"Seriously? You have to leave town? What? Did he hit you? Dud! Dudley!" Dudley Corso was Liz's husband.

He probably wasn't even home. It was a weekday, after all.

"What are you calling him for?"

"I'm sending Dud into New Haven to the stomp the living tar out of Timothy."

"Tim didn't hit me. I lost my job. I'm headed to Tennessee to see about another one."

"Oh. Shit. Sorry. I'm guessing that the committee didn't care for the changes in your research project. You little rebel, you."

"Go ahead, give me the needle. I deserve it."

"So why leave him? Why not just take him with you?"

"I don't think he'd leave his job. He works for his father's company. The great, grand Lowell company. It's one of those generational family things, you know. I think they started it back in the Middle Ages or something."

"You know," and she looked at Leah over the tops of her glasses, "he might just give it all up for you, if you asked him to."

"Maybe. Or maybe he'd talk me into staying here, jobless, career-less. He might guilt me into it or seduce me into it."

"Because you're so weak willed."

"That's right. Give it to me good."

They didn't say anything for a minute. Just listened to the sounds of the neighborhood, birds, cars, a dog barking somewhere and the dripping of the hose.

"There's also this," Leah said.

"What?"

"I cheated on him."

Liz dropped the hose and her mouth fell open.

"Go ahead. Say it."

"Say what? I don't know what to say. I mean other than, are you fucking kidding me? What, what, how in the hell? I mean. Shit."

"Shit is right."

"Uh, uh, why?"

"He's sort of the anti-Timothy."

"The anti-Timothy. The *anti*-Timothy. I'm guessing you mean ugly, poor, and bad in bed?"

"Well, poor anyway."

Liz shook her head.

"Look. I've heard all about Timothy. The face, the body, the sex. The money. Okay, so he's perfect. Wait. Did he cheat on you first? Cause, seriously, that would—"

"No. I don't know what happened. Okay, yes I do. I just realized one day that I don't trust the paradigm. Man, woman, marriage. Children, sacrifice, socially constructed roles. Husband, wife. You know?"

Liz did an exaggerated double take and then stood up and spread her arms and turned in a circle.

"You mean, this?"

"I'm not criticizing this."

"It sure sounds like you are."

"I just mean—I don't know. Why is it mandatory? Why aren't there more options?"

"Like, uh, not get married, have your own place, your own bank account, and keep Timothy and Mr. X as boy toys, like a vibrator on your bedside table?"

"Wow. Just wow."

"On top of which, I get that you have doubts. Sure. How is cheating on Timothy the answer to that?"

"I guess I was trying to, I don't know, break up with him?"

"Is that a question? Are you asking me?"

"I don't know. I. Don't. Know."

"Okay, fine. You don't want Timothy. You don't want Mr. X."

"Quentin."

"Quentin. Wait. Quentin? Never mind. But that's not all there is to this, is it? Something else is going on, no?"

"No. I mean, yes. What I've got to do—well, I just can't take Timothy with me. Or Quentin. Or anybody. I don't think. No. That's not in the picture. I can't take anybody with me. I don't even really know what it is that I'm doing, what it is that I've done."

"Can I summarize it for you?" Liz smiled.

"Please don't."

"You've dragged yourself out of a burning orphanage, pulled yourself up from a GED to a Ph.D.—from Yale, for Pete's sake—you've received prestigious grant money to study sacred places around the world. And then didn't. How am I doing so far?"

"Feel free to stop now."

"You met the man of your dreams—a rich, handsome, well-spoken God of Orgasm, if your pornographic reminiscences are to be believed—who offered you love, marriage, the magnificence of the material world, but you're just not a material girl."

"You can stop any time now."

"You destroyed your reputation at Yale, lost your job, quit your man, tried on another man for size. I'm only assuming just the one," she continued, "hidden your car, and now are about to jump on a plane to some Confederate university to teach Intro to Religion to a bunch of snake handlers and strychnine drinkers—"

"—now you're being ridiculous—"

"—and you still haven't pulled your grandmother out of that old folks' home."

"Ouch."

"Sorry."

"That one hurt."

"Yeah, well, let's forget Timothy for a minute. Forget everything you've done so far, good and bad. Let's just forget it all. What are you going to do about Effie?"

Hm. Good question.

CHAPTER TWO

Merk this in your mynde.
Lydgate, Horse, Goose & Sheep

Effie Rabren braced herself in the open door, facing the prairie. She heard it, but she didn't see it. Effie was a small, blind woman with thin gray hair and a narrow face. A long nose bore a faint, star-shaped scar across the bridge. She was gaunt, rail-thin—thin as a dime. Her round, owl-like eyes were gray and shadowed. She felt the wind against her face, heard it rustling past, but nothing out there seemed unusual. Alice had always said Effie's other senses were sharper than most people's.

"You smell a body before they ever ring the doorbell," she liked to say.

But the truth was, sixty-five years ago when she lost her sight, nothing like that happened. Her other senses hadn't sharpened—at least not in any way she could tell. More like she grew another sense to take sight's place. Not that all the senses in all creation could have stopped the random juggernaut that was the story of her life. Nor would it have stopped her from reaching that moment when the last card in her hand was to move into this retirement home on the edge of the tall grass prairie.

She felt around for one of the rocking chairs. The porch was wide and warm, and the dust slid around under her feet on the painted boards. No way to keep it clean, what with the workings of wind and prairie and the generally poor work ethic among the cleaning folk. Not that she minded. Her room was clean enough.

She missed Alice. Alice had taken her in after Effie's only child Connie and her husband were killed in the fires of '02. Effie's own husband, Butler had died some years before that. Her poor brothers, Abel and Trask, had both been killed long, long ago, in the war. Abel was killed at Midway in '42 and Trask in Italy in '44. All that was left of her family was her granddaughter, Leah who was studying up at Yale College in the northeast. Sometimes she let herself cry for everything she had lost. Nothing wrong with a little self-pity as long as it didn't become your defining quality and wasn't what you were known for...or remembered for.

The home wasn't terrible, as many old folks' homes were. The food was good. The staff were nice. The residents were mostly quiet. They played cards or board games, watched television and followed their stories. When she wasn't on the porch listening to the prairie, Effie would sit in the recreation room, listening to the slap of the cards, the rattling of the dice, the foolishness in the words of the actors on the television. On some afternoons Mr. Elias Eno played the old upright piano in the rec room. Soft, slow, ethereal tunes. Nothing Effie ever recognized. She thought he might be making them up as he went. He never seemed to hit a wrong note. No way to ask him. He was lost in dementia. Never spoke a word. Never left his room except for meals and to play the piano in the afternoon. The home always smelled like baking bread because they did bake their own bread. Good bread, at that. All in all, it wasn't the worst place for one's final act.

No, her other senses had not grown keener when she went blind. What had really happened, truth be told, was that her *marking* had gotten stronger. That's how she thought of it— marking. Sometimes sound would reach in through her ears and mark something on her brain, like chalk on a blackboard. Now it was true that even before she went blind, she had heard things, heard strange things in strange ways. But whether that was marking or not, well, she just couldn't say. It was so long ago.

She had gone blind when she was thirteen. For three days prior to her first womanly time, she heard something approaching, coming to her or, more terribly, for her, out of the sounds and sights and smells of her parents' horse ranch where she grew up, coming to her through the taste of food, the smell of frying bacon, the soft cotton of her clothes. It was a sound like a thousand needles dropping on a tile floor or a field of grasshoppers screaming. When her period came on that third day, Effie went completely blind.

In that moment, beyond the panic, terror and disbelief, it was as if someone turned up the volume on her *marking*. Marking was a kind of hearing, but not so much like it was coming into her ear. It was more like a pressure that was inside her, in her head, just above her mouth and behind her nose somehow.

Now—after her blindness, after her first period—she knew things. She knew what her mother was thinking about cooking for supper. She knew when Mr. Carpenter from up the road was going to show up unexpectedly. She *marked* when a colt was coming or when a mare had gotten into some Johnson grass. Her father, hands caked hard by dirt, and rough sweat-stiff clothes smelling of pipe tobacco, held her in his arms in the evenings after supper, whispering cowboy ballads to her and listening to her *markings* about the ranch.

He took seriously every single thing she said, even if some of her warnings came to nothing. He had once ridden the full fifteen miles of north fence when she told him a horse was caught in the wire. There was no horse, but near the end of the day, in the flaming last red light of the sun, he did come upon a spot near a stand of pines where he had once freed a horse caught in that very wire back around the time Effie was born.

He never doubted her. And whatever he believed about the truth and the source of her *marking*, he kept it in his quiet heart and prayers.

Her mother, Jessie, though, was inconsolable. The tragic coincidence of womanhood and blindness in the person of her one and only daughter stole a treasure of great price from her. Her sweet mother, Jessie, of the light eyes, the wheat-colored hair, the sun-browned skin, had been born sometime just after 1900, came of age in the Great Depression, found her cowboy, Jason Dalton, and had Effie late at nearly forty years old! She vowed her daughter would not endure the poverty and deprivation she herself endured. Effie and Jason worked hard and wrestled their ranch and home out of nothing but the thorns and thistles that constituted the biblical wasteland of west Texas. And now her child, her only daughter, would be blind!

When Jessie would pull Effie onto her lap and hug her with all her might, the agony her mother bore poured into Effie and seemed to fill her stomach and lungs with a cold, hard pain.

Effie spent years trying to convince her mother that blindness had not ruined her life but had made her grateful for all the good things she had and what her parents had provided. Effie did all the things a young woman with sight could do. She finished high school, dated, and fell in love with and married a good man, the inestimable Butler Rabren.

She had her own sweet child named Connie. Even so, despite the long years and the distance between them, she could still feel her mother's pain. When her parents had driven to El Paso and Jessie held baby Connie for the first time, she wept as if unleashing Noah's flood. Effie *marked* the moment, when grandmother met granddaughter. She didn't mark her mother's joy, but grief, brutal ice-cold grief.

Effie thanked the Lord that her mother had passed before Connie did. If Jessie had been forced to carry the weight of her granddaughter's death on top of everything else—ah, it was just as well. No parent should outlive a child, much less a grandchild. Effie had learned the bitterest truth in the life of the faithful. The Lord is sparing with his blessings and mercies.

On the other hand, Effie had gotten no inkling that her daughter and her daughter's man would be killed. She had not *marked* that. *Why not?*

She had been living with them, first in Texas and then in Oklahoma, after her own Butler had died of an aneurism back in '96.

Connie's man, Tom Grove, was an agronomist or agriculturist or some such. Studied plants, is what he did. Before he met and married Connie, he had taken his doctoral degree in botany and hied himself off to South America somewhere to study plants. He had theories, wild theories, crazy theories, really. Lord, the Antinomian heretics had nothing on that boy. He would sit on the porch during an evening with Connie and her, talking a blue streak about how the plant world was awake, how it was as rife with good and evil as much as the human world, maybe even more so. Professor Grove had been let go from the prestigious University of Texas at Austin (for spouting just such foolishness, Effie suspected) and found his way to Oklahoma State University where he got in with a group there working to make the wheat better…more nutritious or sturdier or some such.

Tom Grove kept returning to South America over the years. He was always tight-lipped about whatever he was doing there. It didn't have anything to do with wheat. Effie knew that as surely as she knew her own name. On his last trip, he brought back some plants Effie knew he didn't have any business having in his possession. She thought he probably smuggled them in. She heard Tom telling Connie not to mention the plants to anyone.

Secret plants? And what exactly would that be about?

Late one afternoon, she and Connie sat under the elm tree, while Leah rode her bike up and down the driveway.

Effie lifted her nose in the air and said, "Do you smell that?"

"Course I smell it, Mama. You'd have to be dead and buried not to smell it."

"Well, what is it?"

Connie sighed.

"I think it's those damn South American plants."

"The who?"

"Something Tom got from Bolivia. He says he's crossed them with something else, though he didn't say what. From what he says, it's the crossing that makes the stink. And can I just say, I think he likes the smell?"

"Likes it? Lord oh mighty. Where is he keeping them?"

Connie said, "He's planted them on the south side of the house."

"Mm. That is quite the stink."

"It's worse at night. They're right outside our window, and Tom likes to keep the window open while he sleeps so—"

Well, the plants got the lion's share of Tom's attention, to the point where he was ignoring his duties at the university.

Effie overheard him and Connie one night arguing the point. Connie said that she was tired of making excuses when the Ag department called looking for him. And just what was it he was doing standing there for half a day, staring at those damn plants? It wasn't like he was even tending them— watering, hoeing, and whatnot—he just stood there staring at them.

Later on, Tom seemed to rouse himself from whatever had gotten into him. He packed up Connie, and they drove north with several of the professors from his work to see some wheat fields where they'd been sowing the seeds that they'd somehow modified in their god-forsaken laboratories. Mrs. Driscoll from the Lutheran church came and stayed with her and Leah, cooking and watching out for things. Connie and Tom were to be gone for a week; but, of course, they never came back.

On the fifth day, Mrs. Driscoll got a phone call. Something was wrong, but she didn't say anything until that night, after Leah ate her supper and had gone to bed. She told Effie that Tom and Connie had been killed in a fire, a wind-blown wildfire that swept through the wheat field that they and some other college folk had been inspecting.

Effie had a hard time imagining such a thing. Mrs. Driscoll turned on CNN and eventually the coverage got around to the tragic wildfire that had swept through northern Oklahoma. Over five hundred homes and more than a hundred thousand acres destroyed in less than two days. The fire was driven by forty mile an hour winds and the flames overtook people before they could get moving. There was tens of millions of dollars in damage.

Effie asked her to turn the television off.

There was a bad scene when Child Protective Services arrived two days later. Mrs. Driscoll had called them. Reluctantly, Effie supposed, *what else could the good woman have done?* She couldn't come and live with Effie and Leah herself. She had her own family to look out for.

Leah cried and said she wanted to stay with her grandmother. The child told the lady from the state that she'd just lost both her parents and now she was going to lose her grandmother too. Of course, the lady had no response for that. There was just nothing for it.

Effie thought that, while there is no good time to lose one's parents, thirteen seemed a particularly bad one. Right on the verge of womanhood, adulthood, woman but still child, independent but still needy, smart but really dumb at times. Effie had been the same age when she lost her sight. It hadn't destroyed her, but that was only because she hadn't let it. She had something to prove. To her mother, mostly. Her mother who was thoroughly ruinated by Effie's blindness.

Who did Leah have to prove anything to? What would be her motivation to overcome this tragedy?

The lady from the state said that she was willing to listen to any reasonable ideas the child or Effie had; but, of course, they had none. The lady was right. But that didn't make it right.

In the end, she and Leah said goodbye on the porch of the rented house in the flat little neighborhood north of Berry Creek. Leah cried all the way to the lady's car and Effie could hear her crying even after the door was shut. She thought she heard it even after they had driven off and left her on the porch with her suitcases, waiting on her friend Alice to come and fetch her. Laying down her last card.

She couldn't really hear the child crying, of course. She *marked* it though. Leah cried the whole trip. Effie just knew it.

The wind shifted. She smelled those plants.

Though she had no business doing so, Effie made her way around the side of the house to where Tom had planted them.

Up close, the stench was wretched.

There was a tool shed in back of the house. It would be pure luck if she could find it. She felt around the cool, musty interior until she put her hands on a hoe. She uprooted the three plants and chopped at them like they were snakes. Whatever sap was inside them reeked to high heaven. Satisfied that they were in small enough pieces, she kicked them around in the dirt, trying to separate the pieces as if they might reassemble if left to their own devices. She'd have burned them if she trusted herself not to burn down the whole world.

As if the whole world hadn't burned just a week ago in a massive wheat field in Oklahoma.

CHAPTER THREE

In imitating the exemplary acts
of a god or of a mythic hero,
man detaches himself from profane time
and magically re-enters the Great Time,
the sacred time.
~Mircea Eliade

Timothy stood in the empty back bedroom. Nothing but some dirt spilled from one of those stupid dying plants of hers. He pulled the spoon from his pocket.

What a sad sack I am, he thought, *carrying this thing around like it was her picture.*

It was a message. It was a message as surely as this empty room was a message. *How did she get out of here so quick?* He had only worked half a day that day. He had planned to take her to the symphony that very night. Shostakovich. He still had the tickets, useless now, in the same pocket with the freaking spoon. The freaking bent spoon. *What a loser!*

He loved her. He did. She loved him, he was sure. Wasn't he? True, he didn't have his family's money anymore. But she didn't know that. Did she? Would that matter to her? *I should know at least that much about her. I thought I did. Do I know anything about her?*

He had quit the family firm, Lowell and Sons, when his father informed him about the Madrid situation and that he, Timothy, would be going to Madrid. For a year or more, if his father had his way.

But Timothy was not going to Spain for a year or more. He was not going to work his fingers to the bone trying to straighten out the mess his brother Eddie had made there.

In just three short months, Eddie had turned a smooth-running operation into a shambles. And now his father just assumed Timothy would go and fix everything.

No, forget "assumed." His father had instructed him to go. Just straight up told him to go! Not *"would you be willing to, could you help me out here, your brother's made a mess, and I need you."*

No, just go.

Not *"I don't want to interfere with your plans, I don't want to disrupt your life, but please do this for me. I need you too, son."*

No. Nothing like that. Just a straightforward command as if he were an employee, not a family member...not his son.

It hurt to remember how he had simply turned and walked away, packed the few personal items from his office—hurt to imagine his father uncomprehending, confused that Timothy would walk out, like an employee. Not understanding that he, Timothy, his own son, was someone with every God-given right to say no.

He spoke to his father by phone when he quit. He told him that he would make his own way now.

"I'm not your favorite son, I know, but I am your son, not some worker bee at your disposal."

"That's not fair," his father had said. "I don't have favorite children. I've treated—"

But Timothy cut him off.

"I've cleaned out my office. I won't be back in," and with that he hung up.

Checking his bank account online, two weeks later, he saw that, while his salary had not been stopped from direct deposit, the amount had been cut. Drastically cut.

Doing some quick numbers in his head, he saw they were giving him in the neighborhood of thirty thousand a year. A waiter's salary, an assistant manager at a fast food restaurant. He could just live on it.

Well, not him, but somebody could just live on it. He hadn't touched the money. He'd opened another account and just let the "salary" pile up.

When he got a call from the IRS, he understood that his father hadn't done this. Timothy wasn't getting a salary. He'd been terminated, just as he'd requested when he quit.

The money going into his account was not from the payroll department at Lowell and Sons, but from a more generalized fund, the corporate equivalent of a Petty Cash drawer. Meaning, of course, that no Social Security or Medicare or taxes of any sort had been taken out of the money. It was just being dropped as a lump sum into that account every month. Which meant two things. One, Timothy wasn't clearing anywhere near thirty thousand a year; and two, he would have to arrange to pay all that tax withholding which the firm wasn't doing. The money was not worth the effort, trouble and time it would take him.

The money wasn't a settlement. It was a punishment, which meant it didn't come from his father. More likely, his father had told his younger brother, Edward, Jr. to set up some payment for Timothy, and this was Eddie's idea of a joke.

That little shit.

Little Eddie—boy, Eddie hated that moniker. Thus, Timothy used it incessantly.

Eddie had been his parents' favorite. And why not? To start with, he was the baby. There'd been Andrew, then Timothy, and finally Edward.

Edward the Second, apparently destined to be the scion of a great New England family, one that could trace its ancestry back to the court of Elizabeth the First. Great fortunes spun out in such wonderfully American enterprises as whaling and lumber and railroads. A legacy in need of perpetuation; but not by sons. No, by one son. Three sons would have diluted the power. His father hadn't been unkind about it, but he'd been clear. There is no possibility of greatness in three, since no triumvirate in history had lasted. Two Roman attempts ended in murder and dissolution, the apostolic era ended in the middle of the New Testament, and the French in the Terror.

Look at Lear, his father had said, sanely.

No, in this family, one would rule. And for some reason, incomprehensible to Timothy and Andrew, the one was Little Eddie.

Isn't the first son usually the namesake? Andrew, the eldest, had asked this, rhetorically, of Timothy when Andrew was thirteen and Timothy eleven. This occurred at Little Eddie's eighth birthday celebration. To call it a party would have been to damn it with passive-aggressively faint praise.

Timothy had answered, *Yes, that's usually the way.*

It occurred to him—though he never mentioned it to his brother—that their father might have taken one look at the newborn Andrew and thought, *No, not this one*, and so gave him the grandfather's name instead. Then, when he himself was born, the old man must have thought again, *No, not this one either.* It wasn't until Little Eddie arrived that their father finally looked at a child and said, *Yes, this is my namesake, my legacy bearer, the golden child. Was that how it happened?*

Edward Jr. had been fast tracked into Harvard, before his junior year in high school. Eddie was a good student—brilliant, if truth be told. Smarter than he or Andrew, but it had taken a fair amount of the old man's money to grease those particular wheels. And, to his credit and his father's pride, Eddie did it all in three years. When Eddie graduated, *magna cum laude*, Timothy was still in the Yale MBA program.

The little shit.

Well, for all his brilliance, for all his grades and his *magna cum laudes*, he couldn't pour piss out of the proverbial boot in the business world. Turns out, little Eddie was lazy, more interested in fine champagne and brainless blondes than in making sure the numbers added up. Eddie liked the Lowell money but couldn't be bothered to keep the enterprise going. He had fouled the waters in the New Haven office and, for some reason only the gods on Olympus could discern, Father had sent him to handle things in Spain.

What was the old man thinking?

Timothy knew enough people in Connecticut that he could make a decent living consulting in their various business concerns without his family's money. Money was not his concern.

Was it Leah's? Is that why she left? More to the point, where was she?

Timothy had a childhood friend, Maxwell Thornton, now on the tenure track at Yale. Max was in the English department rather than Religion, but gossip flowed freely across campus, so Timothy invited him to lunch to see what he might know. He reserved a good table at Zinc, arrived early, and waited. They had never been especially close—perhaps they weren't even friends anymore. As Maxwell threaded his way between the tables, Timothy took him in: handsome, with sand-colored hair, a strong jaw, and broad shoulders—like a quarterback out of a college comedy.

"Great to see you, Tim."

Maxwell Thornton dropped into the chair opposite him and picked up the menu. He's taking his time, looking for the most expensive item, Timothy thought. What the heck? What could an associate professor's salary be? Plus, Timothy had picked Zinc for the very purpose of loosening Maxwell's tongue.

"You too, Max."

They were sitting at the front window, and Timothy was watching the lunch crowd walking up and down Chapel Street.

"Have the Hangar Steak. It's really good."

"I'm thinking the Scottish Salmon Salad."

"It's good too."

"You're looking well, Timothy."

"I'm trying to find out—"

Maxwell cut him off.

"I hear you left the family business," he said in a very matter of fact tone.

"You make it sound so movie-of-the-week."

"That's how rich people look to those of us trapped among the hoi polloi."

"How's that?"

Maxwell looked over the menu at him.

"I don't mean anything by it, old boy. You're all locked up behind tall gates and ivied walls and fantastic topiary. The rich are different."

"Fitzgerald, right?"

"Sure. Why not."

"And is this how Yale English professors talk? Clichés and cribbed quotations?"

Timothy could feel the color rising in his neck. He tried to swallow it down with the next drink of water. Was he going to be drawn into an argument and lose his chance to find out about Leah?

"Immature writers imitate—"

Now Timothy cut him off.

"— and mature writers steal, yes, I've got that."

"T.S. Eliot."

Timothy shook his head.

"Fine. Look, I need to ask you something."

"One of the irritating things about the rich," Timothy sighed, "is that they don't really get it. Their experience of life is incomplete. All the hard things—the self-doubt, the search for love, the betrayals of friends—are magnified in ways you, Timothy, can't imagine, because they're all compounded by the constant worry over money."

Timothy shifted in his chair.

"And I'm not talking about the desperately poor. I don't try to pretend I know their lot. Not that I can't imagine. I just don't want to. I'm talking about ordinary people, rich by any global standard, who cannot pass a day without putting their own issues onto the back burner so that they can worry over money. Because the things that can go wrong in your life over money are so much more devastating to your life as a whole than whether or not your girlfriend is badmouthing you behind your back or the servants forgot to pick up your dry cleaning."

"Are you trying to piss me off?"

"Not at all. Why would I do that to an old friend. Who's paying for lunch. I hope."

"Right."

Maxwell sighed.

"Right. I'm trying to point out to you why I might resort to cliché to ask about your quitting the job. I cannot relate to whatever issue would drive you to leave the 'family business', if you'll forgive me. Clearly, it was not money. You see, every decision I make must include some consideration of money."

"That's not true."

"Ah, but it is. Even accepting your lunch invitation. How did you get here?"

"My car."

"I walked."

"You walked what? Half a mile, a third?"

"That's not the point."

"Clearly!"

"Why didn't you walk? It's good for you, you know."

"I was across town. Are you kidding me?"

"Now, I'm assuming you're here to talk about Leah."

"Wh—!"

"Well, you're not going to win this. I'm not letting you turn my innocent comment into an indictment of unearned wealth," Maxwell smiled.

"You're not letting me?"

"So—Leah?"

"What makes you think I'm interested in Leah?"

"Let's not play this hand. Just lay down your cards."

"Okay. She's gone. I don't know where she is or what she's doing. She didn't even leave a note. She left—a bent spoon."

"A bent spoon?"

"In the middle of the dining room table. I guess it's a symbol."

"No. It's a sign."

"What's the difference?"

"I don't have time to do a seminar on semiology but suffice it to say that the spoon doesn't *stand* for something but *signifies* something."

"What?"

Maxwell shrugged.

"I don't know. And, if you're about to ask, I don't know where she is either."

"I didn't think so. But I think something might have happened at work, something that made her leave town."

"Because she couldn't just be leaving you, right?"

Timothy couldn't think of a reply. His mouth was open, but—nothing. He ducked his head. *Of course, she could just be leaving him. Obviously, she could. But I can hope, right?*

"Sorry. But that is a possibility, right?"

Timothy hated to let Maxwell in, but he said, "It was as close to a perfect setup as I have ever been in. I loved her. She loved me. Things were great. I thought we were headed for—I don't know."

"Happily ever after?"

"Do you *have* to be a shit? Is it compulsory with you?"

"Verbal witticisms. These are what I have instead of brilliant originality."

"Whatever."

"Right. Not about me. So. There are several narratives floating around about Leah's departure. Some are sufficiently ludicrous as to merit no rebuttal, but, all right. What I've heard is that after she got the Ph.D., she took a post-doctoral grant to travel and do more research and expand her dissertation into a book. Her area of study, as I'm sure you know, was sacred places. The idea was that she would visit some if not all of the sacred places she wrote about in her dissertation, get pictures, local interviews, whatever, and make a real book out of it."

"That's true. She did that. She was gone nine months."

"Uh—no. She did not. Tim, she took the money and did something else with it. One of the narratives suggests she is being sued by the University to recover the grant money, and that her academic career is over."

Timothy took a deep breath. *Wha...?*

"That's one narrative," Maxwell continued. "Another is this. She changed the parameters of the research. It's entirely possible that the grant committee's complaints may be merely procedural, and that while they probably won't fund her ever again and she'll never be welcome back at Yale, there shouldn't be any serious academic or financial consequences."

"Changed the parameters?"

"Here's where a third narrative might begin to emerge, palimpsest-wise."

"Huh?"

"The parameter she changed was from 'sacred' to evil'."

"Sacred to—"

"Yeah, evil."

"Evil."

"And the story goes that she has gone full wiccan or black magic or something."

"What?"

"That she's dressed in all black and conducting rituals with her research."

"Get out."

"I agree. I'm just the teller here. Three narratives diverged in a wood."

"Again, get the fuck out."

"Final narrative," and here Maxwell took a deep breath.

His faced softened just a bit though Timothy may not have noticed.

"The department found out she was sleeping with one of her students."

Timothy laughed, but Maxwell did not.

Timothy said, "You're serious. You think she was cheating on me?"

"I don't have a thought about it. Wait. No. I take that back. I do not think she was cheating on you, old son. But rumors in the Religion department say she was having an affair with a poetry student, Quentin somebody. Now I've seen this Quentin fellow. He hasn't been in any of my classes, but I know enough of him to know that Leah was not sleeping with him. Okay?"

Maxwell did, in fact, not know that. He doubted it, but who really knew? He liked Leah. He liked her a lot more than he liked Timothy. He believed Timothy had gotten colossally lucky in finding her. *Fucking rich people.* He simply believed that Leah had better taste than to take up with a smelly, half-assed poetry student.

Maxwell cleared his throat.

"So, here's what I know for sure: she's gone. The religion department has washed their hands of her. Wherever she is, she's not coming back here."

"She's been blackballed?"

"I don't think that's the word, but yes. She changed her field of research from sacred places to evil places. The department just wasn't interested in that, and they cut her loose."

"Sacred? Evil? I don't see the difference."

"You don't?" Maxwell smiled.

"I mean, obviously there is a difference. What I'm saying is that if you're going to say that there are places that are somehow inherently sacred, which I take to mean inherently good, and that they are sacred and good *in and of themselves* and not just what people think of them, well then, why not places that are inherently evil? Why wouldn't they let her change her focus. You know, shift the focus of her research. What do they care?"

"It's enough that they do. So, wait. Are you saying that you do not believe a place can be sacred or evil, other than people believe them to be so?"

"Duh. Yeah. Are you kidding? We're educated people, Andrew, not eighth century mystics. The universe, this world, is material. No?"

"No."

"No? Did you just say no? For God's sake, man, you're an Ivy League educated person."

"For whose sake?"

"That's a figure of speech. I don't believe in God, or spirits, or ghosts, or voodoo, or anything else like that. And don't tell me that you do."

"How arrogant do you think I am? Do you imagine that I'm going to sit here with my Ph.D. in literature, *literature* mind you, and suggest that I understand the universe? I'll admit that I'm not much for faith as it's practiced by most of the major religions, but I'll tell something I do know—there is good and there is evil in the world, and those things are not limited to the choices of human beings."

"I don't know what to say to that. I'm flabbergasted."

"Good. Because I don't want to debate it with you. I'm hungry and here comes our food."

After Maxwell had tasted his salmon, he nodded approvingly and said, "Do you know the word 'numinous'?"

"No. I don't think so."

"You should look it up. And by the way, you do know that Leah believes in good and evil, don't you?"

"So?"

"Nothing. Just wondering, how will you raise the children?"

* * * * *

Almost two years they had been together when she disappeared. A full year while she finished up her dissertation. Another year, or a little less, traveling on a grant from the Religion department. She'd kept him at arm's length at first. Well, they'd kissed. Six months in, they had lain together on his bed watching Netflix, their sides pressed together, their hands entwined. He had put his hand under her shirt and promised her the world, but she was nothing if not a realist.

"That's your—let's say 'desire' talking. You'd say anything to separate me from my panties right now."

"Yes. I want you. I'm a guy, what do you expect?"

"Exactly this."

"That's not fair. This is more than lust. I feel something for you, Leah Grove. You feel something for me, I know it."

"I do."

"Then what's the problem?"

"'The problem?' You think there's a problem. You think that there is some knotty issue in my psychology that's holding my pants up? And what problem would that be?"

"I—"

"Maybe I'm repressed, or have some daddy issues, or maybe a priest—"

"Okay, let me interrupt you here. I misspoke. There is no problem."

"You're right there's no problem. The 'issue', if you want to think of this that way, is that I decide. I, the woman, decide. You never decide. You can ask, but you have no rights here. You think because we have gone out for a few months that you can 'expect' something from me? I'm not sorry to say that you have no expectations."

She sat up. His bedroom was nice. Much nicer than hers. Real wood floor, cream-colored walls that might have adorned a church in Florence, with museum quality prints and some local artists. The place looked like a decorator had done it, though she knew it was his work. She did love him for that. He had taste.

"Look," she said as she got up off the bed. "This thing is at an end. This whole male, I must conquer and plant my flag and my seed in this territory and make it mine—it's over. Yes, we may be a generation or two from its complete death but hear me. Women are learning that this world is ours. We have what you want. You have to ask us. Yes, some of you may still beat and rape us, but not for much longer. God created humans, but Samuel Colt made them equal. And intelligence will win out anyway. Smart men already know we're in charge. Haven't you read Frederick Barthelme? Your power grabbing, possession fetish, whatever...is laughable. We're laughing. That's your big fear, isn't it? Women laughing at you. At your bodies, at your antics, your posturing, your dumbass show-offing. You know it better than we do: the limp dick is the flag of female revolution."

"Wow. I don't know what to say."

"Then don't say anything. Because there's nothing to say. Just understand that the paradigm is dead. So, yes, I'll move in here. We can play house. But don't start talking marriage. Don't mention children. Don't offer me any career guidance."

"I just want to take care of you."

"Are you kidding me? Have you been listening?"

"I can buy a house near the school. You can finish your book, start teaching, continue your research, and I'll handle everything else."

"You mean the money, right? Because I'm sure you don't mean the cleaning, the cooking and the diapers."

"I can do that."

"And work?"

He knit his brows.

"Ah. Of course. So, when you say, you'll take care of me, you mean your parents' money will take care of me."

"I suppose you're right to doubt me."

"I don't doubt you. If you say you'll do it, I'm sure you will.

When she got back from her travels, she was different. She was worried about something, but she wouldn't say what it was. She wouldn't even admit she was worried. Things were fine between them. After so much time apart, their lovemaking was off the chart. She was fairly insatiable. She went off to work every day. Now, of course, he knew that wherever it was she went, it was not to work in the usual sense.

And then she was gone.

Not a word. Just a bent spoon.

* * * * *

After his lunch with Andrew, Timothy went back to his house. He looked at all the things he had around him. Nothing meant anything to him without her. What did she care where his money came from? And what if he had told her he no longer had money from his family? That he was earning his own way. Would she think differently of him?

So, he had a secret, and she had a secret. So what? She had lost her job, and he had quit his. Again, so what?

But why didn't she tell him?

Or, conversely, why didn't he tell her?

A poetry student? One of her students? Surely not.

In truth, he didn't tell her because he didn't think it was a permanent situation. He had honestly thought his father would call him. That his father would apologize, admit he was wrong, admit he favored Eddie over him and pull him back into the fold of family and money.

He didn't, of course.

And all that stuff Maxwell had told him...what was that? Surely, she was right now somewhere working on a way to get back into the good graces of the department and the university. And maybe he could help her. What could he do?

Could he suddenly believe in what she did?

Could he forgive her for fucking somebody else if it came to that?

Wait. He felt dizzy and stumbled to the couch. He lay back and closed his eyes, trying to stop the spinning of the room. Slowly the spinning stopped, replaced by a dull headache. It was all so clear now.

He hadn't believed in her research, in her project. In her.

And she knew it.

All of his women friends had explained to him, in terms ranging from tired patience to angry incomprehension, that Leah had most certainly been insulted by his offer to take care of her. That she had left him in order to show him and the whole world that she needed no taking care of.

But they were wrong—he saw that now. She had left because he didn't believe in what she was doing. If his agnosticism had slipped through when she spoke of sacred spaces, how much more glaring would his disbelief have been if she had confided her desire to seek out and understand places of evil?

Looking at himself through her eyes, he was disappointed.

Surely there was hope. Maybe he could come to understand what she was doing and show her that he respected what she was doing. Maybe he could convince her to come back to New Haven. He could help her pay back the research money the school claimed she had wasted, that she had fraudulently taken from them so that she could do research they had not approved of. He could save her and her academic career. Hell, he could get his father's company to fund her research. She could be an independent scholar.

He got up and went into the bathroom. He dug in the medicine cabinet for some ibuprofen. What could he do now? Maybe he could still save her.

Wait. What am I saying?

* * * * *

He Googled "evil places" and his mind was blown. Jesus, the things people would believe. He read what he assumed were the same things she had read. He browsed through websites both academic and, well, just nutty. He tried not to judge too much, but to see what it was people were looking for here. He followed one link to another and another and found himself on the Amazon site. He searched for books on evil places. There was not much there. He looked at a lot of titles, but nothing seemed to be about evil places in the real world. He was on page thirty-six and about to give up when he found it.

No cover was available. Amazon wasn't selling it, but one of the independent booksellers that sell through Amazon had it available. Timothy had bought books this way before many times. Sometimes the sellers were small bookstores, sometimes just individuals trying to sell off whatever they had lying around or had no more room for, like old college books, grandma's books, and whatnot. Who knew? The sixty-six-dollar selling price drew him up short. *What the hell?* How many books had he bought for a penny plus $3.99 shipping and handling? Obviously, sixty-six bucks was not a fortune. He'd drop that in a second for a good dinner. But for a book?

The title was *The Substantiation of Evil in the Biological World: The War of the Kingdoms.* Clearly, an academic text. It would be dry as dirt, he knew. He clicked the thing into his cart, and two days later ordered it, having found nothing else that seemed appropriate.

Standing at his mailbox and pulling it out of its substantial Federal Express mailing pouch, Timothy had almost thrown it away with the packaging. The newspaper wrapping around it was not taped, and at first, he couldn't distinguish the wrapping from the book itself. He stood over the trash, thumbing the pages. It was less than 50 pages. *More than a dollar a page*, he thought. He left his house and walked down to the community garden park at the corner. A bench near the back was open, so he sat down and began to thumb through the "book," if you could call it that. A breeze freshened and swished the leaves and bushes around.

The book had a hand-drawn cover, some plants, leaves, stems, tendrils all interwoven and slightly menacing like Medusa's hair. The title page and copyright page were hand-lettered, and the author had drawn the copyright symbol by hand as well. There was a table of contents, though none of the chapters had names: Chapter One, Chapter Two. *Why bother?* Some of the pages were hand-written in blue ballpoint and some were typed. It had erasures, white-out, and some words just scribbled out. It had been typed onto notebook paper., back and front, and stapled together!

The author was clearly a madman.

The early pages consisted of a turgid explanation of the Linnaean system of classes for plants, followed by a strangely philosophical discussion of the difference between plant and animal cells that Timothy, quite frankly, could not get the gist of. Then the book took a metaphysical turn.

Any researcher who cared to look would notice the number of plant toxins that seemed "engineered" to ward off humans by killing them. Of the total number of poisonous plants known to botanists, a large percentage of them kill only humans. Let that sink in a moment. The toxins in a frighteningly large number of poisonous plants are aimed directly at humans. Almost any other animal on the planet could eat them and they would be fine, nourished even. These plants only kill us. What kind of engineering is that? Certainly not the hand of God. What but design of darkness to appall if design govern in a thing so small?

Timothy shook his head.

Design: here's a question no researcher will ask: why aren't all mushrooms poisonous? If the toxicity of fungi functions to frighten off predators who might eat them, why are some mushrooms poisonous and others delicious? Wouldn't it make more sense, in evolutionary terms, for all mushrooms to be poisonous? Don't the delicious ones keep encouraging people to eat mushrooms? Or am I asking this the wrong way round? Maybe the whole idea is to NOT to scare us off with poison, but to lure us in with deliciousness. Maybe the good ones are just bait to trick us into putting the poison in our own mouths. How is that for natural selection? Rather than select into a defensive posture, a species that goes on the offense!

What disturbed Timothy was not how nuts the guy was, because he was clearly nuts, but how much sense he was making.

What same forces guide us, for what have we as a species done but wipe out our competition?

And their lovely names: the Latin American death cap, the East Asian brown death cap, the Autumn Skullcap, the Splendid Webcap, the Yellow Clubbed Foot, the Deadly Dapperling, the Chestnut Dapperling, the Deadly Parasol, Yellow Knight, Man-on-Horseback. The Fool's Mushroom. The Eastern North American Destroying Angel, the Western North American Destroying Angel, the European Destroying Angel, the Great Felt Skirt Destroying Angel.

And, of course, Ergot.

Please, as an act of scientific curiosity on your part, take note of how many are described as men: the knight, the horseman, the dapperlings, and the fool. All conscious beings, all beings with will. And the angels! And what if one should hold me against his heart!

What in the world was he reading? Would any of this help him with Leah?

But I digress: Ergot. We all know the most grotesque of the Ergot stories.

In July 1518 The Dancing Plague was a case of dancing mania that occurred in Strasbourg, Alsace. More than 400 people danced for days without rest, and many of those affected died of exhaustion, maybe from strokes or heart attacks. The plague killed twenty people a day for months. They danced themselves to death. No one knew why. We now know it was Ergot poisoning.

Or I should say, it was Ergot himself.

Even the plants we trust. How laughable we are. We trust these things to let us consume them. How disdainfully we destroy them. And, almost every plant food we consume will kill at least some small percentage of our population. Consider the peanut. And those people with an allergy to it. Which is to say the peanut can and does kill people. People today laugh at the folk who once feared the tomato as poisonous, and yet, the tomato is a member of the nightshade family (Solanaceae). Tomato leaves and stems contain the toxin solanine, which, if ingested, causes potentially fatal digestive system problems. The leaves, stems, and green unripe fruit of the tomato plant also contain the poisonous alkaloid tomatine.

And this is not the most egregious.

One might postulate direct action in plants. Is this even necessary? Plants take action. They find a way. Watch a vine, watch it seek, test, retreat, find a way. One might even suggest that in the plant world there is a Will to Power of sorts. And if a plant can take action, isn't revenge an action?

Many voices will arise in disagreement, I know. But surely this next idea will generate the most profound and vociferous scientific rejection in the history of the paradigm: there IS in the plant world, whether individually or in some kind of hive mind situation, a consciousness, *similar to that of animals. Maybe even a kind of self-consciousness.*

I won't belabor the obvious on what constitutes self-consciousness. Let the psychologists and philosophers battle over that one. It is enough to say abstraction, the ability to abstract concepts, to imagine cause and effect toward an end, is enough to make a thing self-conscious. And that is the beginning of evil. No sane person would describe an animal's actions, even those of killing humans, as evil. Because evil is a choice. One must choose evil. There is no other way. Nothing is naturally evil. Even God is not in His nature good or evil. The problem of good and evil? The problem of observation and judgement and choice of action? Well, that has always been the bailiwick and the burden of humankind.

Oh, but what of the natural evils of famine and disease, the natural disasters of hurricane, flood, and fire? I assert that these are not evil, but just bad. Only the arrogance of the self-conscious would find that the world in its intense indifference to human beings is therefore evil. When the natural world kills, it kills out of instinct, out of physical determinism, not choice.

And what would Man do, if he found himself with a virus, an illness, a millstone dragging him down to death. His move to kill that bug: instinct or choice? Or some bizarre amalgam? What a piece of work is Man? What a freak he is. The universe become aware of itself. Or some virus that thinks because it can write poetry it is superior, it is other *than the natural world? No matter. Let us consider this:*

The Earth is a plant world. Plants are the dominant species. Can you imagine that?

The Bible says that God created water first, then Man. As if it were water that was necessary for life. And of course, it is. For plant life. A plant will effectively find water anywhere while a man dies of thirst. Roots, when the ground is dry, will burrow toward moisture, stretching 100 feet from the plant, with an energy that can crack stone as surely as Excalibur. Roots will reach for pipes that Man himself has buried, and they will break those pipes and steal that water. And thus we must conclude plants have intelligence.

No. It's true. While they may or may not have consciousness or self-consciousness, they most certainly have intelligence. Put a vine under a slow motion camera and watch it search for a hold. Our own eyes are too impatient to see its movement but move it does. And not randomly. Turn the vine or move the hold and the plant will turn too and seek that hold. Yes. But how? Does it see? Smell? Place a barrier between the vine and the hold: the vine still knows the hold is there and will circumvent the barrier and find its purchase anyway.

Think on that.

Remove plant life from the Earth and there would be no life. The meat you eat survives on plants before you eat it. On the *underside of leaves all over the world, billions of tiny mouths consume CO_2 and through the magic, the necromancy of photosynthesis (our word, our weak, scientific word) expels the oxygen required for all animal life, including the smartest animal, Man. Thirty million square miles of leaf surface is on this planet. They keep us alive.*

And what if they have grown tired of it? Of this duty to us? How might they eliminate us?

Maybe they would have us dance ourselves to death?

A few years ago] I began a correspondence with a botanist in Oklahoma. He was concerned about the rise in Ergot infestation in U.S. wheat. The Department of Agriculture had been relatively effective in keeping contaminated wheat out of the food supply, but this gentleman was concerned that the incidence was statistically significant. It was rising faster than any of the models had predicted. I was at in South America, studying Ayahuasca. Native shamans and witch doctors used a potion made from the plant to induce religious delirium, resulting in visions and prophecies. This, of course, was nothing new to me. I had already spent a lifetime studying peyote and psilocybin and jimson. But I was taking a new tack, changing the metaphor from the plants opening a door to another world or opening something inside the practitioners. I was considering the idea that the plant itself was speaking to practitioners. The shamans were not being transported. Instead, they were being possessed by the plant itself, and it was the plant that spoke, not some ghost or god, but the plant itself.

How this Dr. Grove got my name, I'm not sure, but when I returned from the jungles to Iquitos, I found his letter waiting for me. He wrote about his work with wheat and with Ergot. Over the course of a year he wrote me several letters. It took him a long time to finally ask what he wanted to ask.

On my next trip to the jungle, I partook of the Ayahuasca potion myself. I was convulsed with sweats and fevers and vomiting for the better part of an hour, after which I was led down to the river and laid in the shallows. As I watched the gray sky behind the intertwined limbs of the overhanging trees, a voice from deep inside my own mind spoke to me and gave me visions. Ergot.

Wait. What. Timothy shook his head and reread the last paragraph. Dr. Grove? No. Surely not. Surely not.

He tried to remember what little Leah had ever told him about her father. He was some kind of professor, wasn't that right? Out in Oklahoma. Studying what? He wanted to say corn or wheat or something, but he couldn't really remember. Her parents had been dead for so long, he hadn't thought he needed to give the issue much attention.

And you wonder why she left, you self-centered shit.

A cloud blocked the sun and a breeze passed over the little garden. He gave a little jerk as a leaf brushed his neck.

The Ayahuasca put something in me. The plant put something in me. On purpose. Willfully. I know how this will sound to my fellow scientists. When the effects of the plant wore off, I was exhausted. I felt I had run a marathon and then had been beaten by a gang of toughs. For a full day, I lay in the shade of a Cyrilla tree and watched the tender blossoms waving against the sky, which in retrospect glowed an odd sulfurous yellow. A native woman occasionally brought me water and fruit; the fruit I could not yet eat.

Late in the day, I awoke from an uneasy dream to find the shaman sitting next to me, staring out into the jungle. The sun was still visible, orange through the dark green of the foliage. He indicated the falling sun with a nod of his head. I stared at the light coming through the trees. It seemed to dance around the trunks and between the leaves. I attributed the vision to the aftereffects of the Ayahuasca. Finally, the shaman spoke.

"Mʉ, ñʉjepacʉ, cavarõ mearocacʉ, meacʉ bajubu mʉ. Que baru caivʉ põeva mʉre pueđarī mearore jíjarãri. Bʉre đajacʉ mʉ mi jabotequiyede põevare. Caivʉ ijãravʉcavʉ đajarãri mearore yópe mi ʉrõpe, yópe ina cavarõ mearocavʉ ne đaiyepe mi ʉrõpe cainʉmʉa."

At least, that's what he seemed to say. I had absorbed some of the dialect, but my translation here is rough. More or less, what he said was that the spirit of the Ayahuasca was now in me. That it would never leave me. That the spirit of the plant and I were now cohabitating, for lack of a better word, the same space. Not, mind you, that the plant was controlling me. This was not a possession in some Judeo-Christian demonic sense, but rather that it was with me. That it would, if I understood the language correctly, walk with me all the days of my life and would dwell with me in the house of my fathers.

What the hell? Timothy thought.

The sun was completely covered now, and the breeze chilled him. He was taking this stuff too seriously. The writer was obviously insane. He scanned the next few pages until he saw the name again.

After this experience, I found the final letter waiting for me from Dr. Grove. The letter asked me directly about my studies with Ayahuasca. I had been hesitant to share my work with scholars in the U.S., inasmuch as a hysterical drug policy cast a pall over all research into what the DEA would describe as a schedule one drug, but when he mentioned Ergot, I was intrigued. This Dr. Grove believed he had found a vestige of intelligence in the Ergot, a sense of purpose, as if it were not an accident of nature that Ergot would attach itself to wheat, but that the Ergot was deliberately seeking out human foodstuffs to blight.

One might say that the scales fell from my eyes or that I had a Road to Damascus moment. My experience with Ayahuasca and the words of the shaman were indeed with me. I could feel the thing behind my eyes, in the linkages and sinews of my limbs. I was more than just myself now. Dr. Grove was proposing...no, not proposing, but considering that he might genetically alter Ergot so that he could ingest a small amount and somehow see its intelligence, its underlying purpose, its teleology, if you will.

Wait. What? Timothy dropped the book into his lap and looked up. The sky was marbled black and gray with thunderheads. The cool breeze was now a chilly wind that scattered the other residents back toward their homes. Her father had wanted to ingest Ergot. That could not be true. First, it had to be a coincidence. This Dr. Grove was not her father. No way. What are the odds? Or let's grant for moment the possibility that the two men were one and the same. The man was a scientist, not a nut. Surely, he wasn't going to deliberately poison himself with Ergot. Ergot! Great God Almighty. He took out his phone and made a note to look up professors at the University of Oklahoma and maybe Oklahoma State. It had to be a coincidence.

The idea, as I understood it, was to synthesize some amalgam of Ergot and Ayahuasca and to find a way to speak with the spirit of Ergot, if such a thing existed. I, by this time, was in full possession of the knowledge of the spirit that lives in Ayahuasca. Let me be clear: the plant mind is not individual. A spirit did not come out of one plant and take up residence in me. There is no such thing as one plant, the way we think of there being one man. No, the idea is closer to that of the hive mind that operates within bee colonies or anthills. But even that is faulty analogy, suggesting many minds working together in a coordinated way to accomplish one goal. The plant mind is not many minds, but one. Maybe a better analogy is the Trinity, wherein three are actually one. Except with the plant mind, thousands, even millions are one. It is said that a forest of pines stretching across hundreds of miles is, in fact, one entity, not individuals working together, but one. One.

And so, Dr. Grove asked me to send him a sample of Ayahuasca, and I did to my everlasting sorrow. For it resulted in his death, and the deaths of his wife and young daughter. I won't go into the details here. One could find all he needs on the objective details of the tragedy in American newspapers. What the newspapers don't say—what they couldn't know—was that the benign spirit of Ayahuasca did not make Dr. Grove burn down his own house with his family inside. It was Ergot. Ergot. What Dr. Grove learned, I assume, is that Ergot (and I will give it the respect of a capital letter now and in the future), Ergot is not a benign thing. Whatever it whispered in the good doctor's ear, I hope it burned with the house and its poor occupants.

A couple of raindrops the size of thumbs struck the page Timothy was reading. That settled it. Leah's father had not burned his house, with his wife and kid in it. Leah's parents had died in a fire, yes, but a wind-fueled fire in a giant wheat field with nowhere to hide. And while her parents were in fact dead, Leah was alive. Timothy stood up and folded the book into his jacket pocket, walked out of the garden and toward the street. A full-on storm was getting ready to break. Nevertheless, he walked away from his house and down the next block. At the corner, he stood with some other pedestrians waiting for the light to change and squeezed his eyes shut, trying to picture Leah's face, and imagine where she was.

God damn it, he thought.

It had started to rain in earnest now. The trees lining the street were whipping in a frenzied wind. He stepped under the shelter of a bus stop and took out his phone. He checked his bank balance: $2,318.45.

Good Lord, I'm broke.

He punched a few buttons and brought up the account into which he'd been siphoning his "salary" from the family firm. $8,500.00. *Okay. Private detective time.*

* * * * *

"I'm not a private detective, Mr. Lowell."

"I'm confused."

To Timothy's surprise, the man had come to his apartment rather than meeting him in an office somewhere. The man was short and round and bald as a roc's egg. He certainly didn't look like a private detective. He said his name was Calvin Tompkins.

"I'm a skip tracer. When you called Whitmore Detectives, it was obvious to them that you don't need a detective. You need a skip tracer."

"And what is that, exactly?"

"I find people. Mostly people who have a court date that some bail bondsman wants them to show up for. You don't need investigation services. You need a skip tracer."

"Okay, fine. I'm looking for a woman. Her name is Leah Grove. She's a—"

"I'm sorry. Let's back up a second. What is your relation to this woman?"

"What?"

"Your relation. Are you her brother, her boyfriend? And why do you want to find her?"

"What difference does that make? And how is this any of your business?"

"I understand."

Tompkins shifted on the couch where he'd planted himself and sunk into the cushions so deeply that Timothy wondered whether he'd have to pull the man to a standing position at the end of their meeting.

"But here's the thing, Mr. Lowell. I don't find women for men who might be looking to hurt them. If this woman is not your relative, if she is in hiding from you, I will not find her for you. I do hope you understand."

Timothy sighed.

"Yes. Of course. I understand. And I appreciate what you're saying. I admire your honesty and your commitment to doing the right thing."

Tompkins said, "Right. So—your relation to the woman, uh, this Leah Grove?"

"Boyfriend, I guess. I thought it was getting very serious. I'm in love with her. I thought—"

"And she? Is she in love with you?"

"Yes. Well, I think so."

"So why did she leave? Is she hiding from you?"

"I don't think so, no. I'm not really sure she's even hiding. Unless it's from the Anthropology Department at Yale."

"The Anthropology Department at Yale. Uh huh. And why would she be hiding from the Anthropology Department at Yale."

"Long story. She left the school under a cloud of some kind. Something about grant money being misspent? Maybe. I don't trust my source on that."

"And your source on that was?"

"Maxwell Thornton. He's a professor of English at the school."

Tompkins was clicking furiously on his device.

"And you don't trust him—why?"

"He's a dick, to be honest."

"Okay. So, any idea where she might be?"

"I can only think that she might be teaching somewhere. Oh! Wherever she is, I'll bet her grandmother is with her now. The lady was in an old folks' home in Oklahoma somewhere, but Leah always talked about bringing her out so they could live together."

"Old folks' home. Oklahoma. Okay. Well, I'll look into it and get back to you ASAP. Did the agency explain my fee?"

CHAPTER FOUR

The Experience of Sacred Space
makes possible the founding of the world:
where the sacred Manifests itself in space,
the real unveils itself, the world comes into existence.
~Mircea Eliade

What foolish things people are, Leah thought as she carried the ladder out onto her balcony.

She had found the ladder in the storage closet. It must have belonged to the previous tenants. The ceilings in the apartment were twelve feet high, so a ladder was probably necessary. Clearly the previous tenants had never found the need to clean the blades of the ceiling fans. Maybe she would do that. Or not. She propped the ladder against the edge of the roof and climbed. Stepping off the ladder onto the Spanish tiles of the steeply pitched roof, she realized for the first time that she was afraid of heights.

Foolish, she thought.

The northern horizon was a stretch of the Cumberland mountains. To the south, the city of Knoxville spouted like a window garden. As she turned toward the east, toward the back wall of the Greymont, a quick wind buffeted her, almost pushing her off balance. She looked at the ladder. What if the ladder fell over? How would she get down? Trapped on this roof was not something she wanted to experience. She certainly didn't want to still be up here when the stars came out, hard in the clear sky.

She could see no end to the grove beyond the wall. A mix of pine, oak and beech. Maybe. Or black cherry. About two hundred yards beyond the fence, one dead tree stood taller than the rest.

Foolish thought.

She knew she had to get there. Something was there. Something was under that tree. Something bad.

Foolish.

She spent ten minutes trying to figure out how to get back on the ladder without falling to her death.

The next morning, she drank coffee on her balcony and stared out over the wall.

Am I kidding myself? All the things I need to get done and I'm out here looking for evil over my back fence?

She also considered why she thought it was that she could "feel" evil now, as if it were a breeze. Or a chill. Had she seen enough evil at this point to have been altered by it? Did she grow a third eye that could see evil?

Or are you just a narcissistic, not-as-smart-as-you-think-you-are egomaniac?

Leah had so much to do. There were still a dozen boxes to be unpacked. Not that she had counted, she hoped no more than a dozen.

You should drive to campus and get a look around. Find your office. For that matter, find out if you even have an office. And for that matter's matter, find out if you still have a job. They may have called Yale and changed their minds about you altogether. Instead, she put on jeans and an old flannel shirt—Timothy's, damn it—and went out into her backyard to find evil.

*****

She sat on the ground next to the wall with her iPad, trying to identify the plants creeping over it. Most of them she found pretty easily. She really got on a roll with the help of a University of Florida website and soon had a list of sixteen different plants, mostly folks would call weeds, though some had pretty flowers.

Plants are amazing, she thought, *finding their way over and under and through a stone wall, clutching at brick, at leaf and stem, lifting through light and spiraling.*

She could find nothing on three of the plants. One was a curling tendril of a vine holding forth a vivid blue flower with notched petals. Another sported a prickly stem with tongue-like leaves, black with veins of red. The last one she couldn't really see. It barely reached the top of the wall. She thought about dragging that ladder down and climbing up to get a better look at it, then thought she might be getting a little carried away. The parts of it she could see, and her imagination of the rest assembled in her mind a deep green plant, almost blue-green, with a spike on top and flowers so nearly baby blue as to appear white. She had the distinct impression that she could smell the flower of this mostly unseen plant, a tart, almost citrusy smell, with an undercurrent of rot. Or maybe the rot reek was coming from the ground, it was hard to tell.

She stood up and brushed off her hands and the back of her jeans. She retrieved her iPad and notebook. She had sketched the leaves and flowers of the plants she couldn't identify. Maybe later she would search some other botanically oriented websites.

*****

After lunch, Leah made up her mind. She locked the door and strode toward the front gate. The thing's electric eye registered her approach and opened the double gates to allow her egress. She had put on her walking shoes, the ones she used to hike the high rocky places of New Haven. She had made up her mind to see the wall from the other side.

She walked through the gates and onto the little street called Lexington Avenue, then a quick left and down toward the stoplight. Crossing Lexington was Coronet Street. It was a larger artery with more traffic. A boulevard, she thought, since it had grassy median dividers down the middle of the street.

Is boulevard the right word for streets with tiny narrow parks in their middles?

Tall gray thunderheads loomed in the eastern sky.

It's going to rain on you, she thought.

The sidewalk was narrow and close to the street. Cars whipped by her, blurs of comic book colors. The woods were on her left and continued as far as she could see up the street. Across Coronet Street, old houses faced her, their once white or cream exteriors faded, green stained from oaks towering above them. In the darkening afternoon, she could see faint lights deep in the downstairs rooms through the front windows.

Leah thought she had walked a goodly mile at least when finally she found a dirt track heading off into the woods. It seemed to be running parallel to the wall, which she now realized would be a mile's trek back through the woods. She walked the two hundred or so yards that she imagined would put her directly behind the apartment complex. She looked for a way in for the undergrowth was Amazon jungle thick. The two ruts that constituted the path looked as if they had not been driven on in a while. When a man touched her on the shoulder, she jumped a foot in the air.

"Sorry, miss."

The man was backing up and doffing his cap. He was short and bald with a gray fringe around his head, and a raspberry birthmark covering his left cheek.

"You look lost, and you didn't answer when I called out."

"Yes," she said, "you got me pretty good. Whoa, my heart is pounding. Look, my hands are shaking. Wait. Where are you going?"

The man had turned and begun his way down the little road. He stopped now and turned.

"I live just yonder."

"You live in here?" Leah looked up at the dark canopy of trees overlaced above them.

"Ya thirsty? C'mon. I got co'colas in the icebox."

A slight bend in the road revealed the man's home…a trailer park, or what was left of one. There were maybe a dozen spots for trailers, though only three seemed to be occupied, another four or five with trailers rotting away on them, and some overgrown spots, just concrete slabs where trailers once parked. Maybe. Even the occupied trailers seemed crowded out by trees and undergrowth. Nowhere was any place you might call a yard to mow or to sit out in. There was a small wooden porch built on the front of one of them, and into this one the man went. The trailers were no more than a few feet off the little road, but it was significantly darker here. No lights were on in the man's trailer. It was as dark as the pit itself.

"I'm Jeremiah Patchett," he said, emerging from the gloom of the trailer's interior and handing her a bottle. It was cold and beads of condensation were already forming on it. She drank gratefully.

"I'm Leah Grove."

"'Grove' is it? That's rich. C'mon up and have a seat."

The ramshackle little porch had a rusty topped table and two lawn chairs. She sat down and put the Coke on the table. She looked around.

"How long have you lived here?"

"Oh. Let's see. Moved here in '76, the year of the bicentennial. This place was full then. All kinds lived up in here. Old folks, families, little kids running around. It was nice. I had just gotten out of the army and was feeling kinda lost and mixed up, you know, the war and whatnot. Thought I'd work a little and keep to myself. This seemed like a good place to do it."

"Keep to yourself."

"I wasn't much of a soldier. Oh, I went to Vietnam, but I didn't care for it."

Leah's eyes widened.

"I wouldn't think so. Who could like such a thing?"

"Oh, I don't mean the war. But you're right, I didn't like that neither. I mean—well, it's just that—shoot. It was too close. Too many people too close together, all sleeping in one hut, eating, showering, making toilets together. I just didn't care for it."

"Gotcha."

"My folks were from out in the country down in Lincoln County. I thought I'd just go home after my service, but by then they were dead. They didn't own nothing outright, so there wasn't no need to go back there. I came here, thinking to live alone in the woods. Like Thoreau. You ever heard of him?"

Leah nodded.

"But then I thought of the trouble of living so far from a grocery store and a barber shop, so I drove around outside the city limits of Knoxville and stumbled upon this place. It was quiet, folks were friendly enough but kept their own counsel, if you know what I mean."

"Indeed I do."

Mr. Patchett stared out at the trees and didn't say anything else for a long moment.

Leah cleared her throat.

"Where did everybody go?"

Patchett shook his head as if waking from a dream.

"Oh, well, you know. They just moved away. Some died, of course. The way of things. Really, though, I think it's these woods."

"The woods?"

A fine mist was sifting through the trees, the air gray and shimmery with it. Leah wondered if she were going to end up walking through the woods in the pouring rain. She wasn't eager to leave the little porch, either to drag herself through the trees and undergrowth toward the wall or to return home the long way.

"Mr. Patchett?"

He turned toward her, and she thought his face constituted a kind of poem or lamentation on the tragic history of the South. Long creases lined the sides of his mouth, brown eyes deep as a muddy river, white beard stubble against his leathery tan cheeks. He stood up. He wore a khaki shirt and pants like a soldier or some kind of delivery man.

"Come with me," he said, and led her around behind the trailer.

There was barely enough room to walk between the back of the trailer and the undergrowth and small trees crowding the property.

"It's a full-time job just keeping the vines from taking over."

There were some hoses on ground, a wheelbarrow with weathered wooden handles propped against the trailer, but the thick encroaching woods had left him only a few feet of what might be called "yard" if you lived in town, but what he had here was just a narrow strip of ground.

"It's a true saying that the place has gone downhill. I had been writing a little history of this trailer park. I started it a long time ago, back when the place was still full. At first, the folks here didn't want to answer my questions, but beer and bourbon on my porch had a way of loosening their tongues. I wrote it all down, who they were, how they came here, who had the places before they did. The births, deaths, marriages, baby with the water on the brain, the drunk whose deck was missing an ace and a jack, the lonely ladies—you know, the novelistic features of the place."

"That's amazing. Did you finish it?"

Mr. Patchett pushed back some foliage, and they stepped out into a little clearing where the ground was burned black, and he shook his head and brushed off his shoulders. He pointed to a spot in the trees, and Leah could make out a place where a trailer had once stood. The concrete apron was split and broken by roots and small trees grown up through it.

"There used to be a trailer right there. A woman lived there. A beautiful woman. I'm not ashamed to admit I loved her. Well, loved from afar, as they used to say. I guess any man in his right mind would have. Oak tree pushed right through the foundation there, you see?"

Leah could see the concrete broken like a wafer at one end, the stump of a tree protruding from it.

"Came right up through the slab and nudged the trailer up so that it sat cattywampus and the lady couldn't live there anymore."

"Did you cut the tree down?"

"After she left, the tree pushed the trailer almost on its side. Somebody finally came and hauled it off for scrap or something. Yeah, I cut it down. I don't rightly know that it was the tree drove her off. She might have had business elsewhere, maybe married somebody who'd put her in a real house. It kindly hurt me a bit when she left, though in truth not fifty words passed between us in all the time she was here. But Lord, she was a sight to see. A treasure."

Leah flashed on Timothy, back in New Haven.

Is he missing you like this? Will anyone ever miss you like this old man misses that woman?

"It wasn't long after she left that I started writing my book about this place."

"Does this little park have a name?"

"It was called The Road of Remembrance Trailer Park."

"That's—ornate."

"This little road that you walked in on is The Road of Remembrance."

"What a nice name for a road."

"At one time folks lived up and down the road, but they all slowly moved away, and sold their land to the TVA or somebody."

"The TVA?"

"Well, somebody like that. Somebody who isn't going to do anything with the land but sit on it until such a time as some money can be made off it."

"So, who owns the trailer park?"

"Say what?"

"Who owns the land that the trailers sit on?"

"Oh. Well, we send our rent checks to some company in Knoxville. Ever oncet in a while they send out letters hinting that they're going to close the place down permanent-like, but nothing ever comes of it."

Mr. Patchett stepped onto the broken foundation of the long-gone woman's former home. He kicked some dead leaves around and then put his foot up on the stump of the tree that had brought down the domicile.

"I don't reckon the tree done it on purpose. Do you?"

"Uh, no. I don't see how. It's just a tree."

Mr. Patchett nodded.

"I don't know. Plants are smarter than you think."

"Really."

"Oh yeah. One of them old Greeks, Aristotle or one of 'em, thought that plants have souls."

"Aristotle."

"Did you know that a climbing plant will change its growth in relation to its support."

"I'm sorry, what?"

"I used to grow pole beans out here when I could keep the ground cleared. You don't have to lead the bean to the pole. A pole bean plant will find the pole you put out for it. Now you might say that's just chance. But if you put the pole in the ground and the next day find that the bean reaching for it, all you gotta do is pull that pole out and put it on the other side of the plant and that bean will turn around and start growing toward the pole that you just moved. Now how does that bean know where the pole is? It was growing right toward the thing and then stops and turns around when you move it. Can it see the pole? I ask you."

"I'm sure there's some reason—"

"Yeah, there's a reason all right. They're smart, them pole beans. You can't trick 'em. Look at these woods. Oncet it was like a park out here. You could wander in these woods all day, see some wonderful things. Not no more. It was like, one day the woods decided to take it all back. The undergrowth came in like kudzu. Ever day closer to the trailers. Soon nobody had a yard. Oh, we tried to fight it off. I come home from work ever day and went at it with a machete. Old Bull Lee what used to live right over yonder in that falling down trailer rented a bush hog and ran it through here, but within two weeks it was plain as the nose on your face that his two hundred dollars was poorly spent. Never saw nothing like it. Ever oncet in a while I'll come out here and burn off this little spot we're standing in. Hell, come back next week and you can watch me burn it again. I can't keep up. What these woods want, they'll have."

For the next half hour, Mr. Patchett guided Leah through the ruins of the trailer park, pointing out the abandoned lots, the collapsing ones, and the two—besides his own—that were still inhabited. She climbed over fallen trees and stood on empty concrete pads while he urged her to be careful.

"What are you doing out here anyway," he finally asked her.

"Well, it's crazy I know, but I wanted—okay, so I live in an apartment complex west of here that backs onto these woods. I wanted to find my way to the wall of the complex and see it from this side."

"Huh?"

"Yeah, I know. I'm not sure what I was thinking."

"I'll tell you right now that you for sure don't want to be lighting out into these woods looking for something you don't know where it is."

"The wall has got to be due west from here. If I walk straight through, I should run right into it, yeah?"

"No. Not necessarily. Have you a compass? How are you going to maintain a westward track when you are constantly going around a fallen tree or a thicket you can't get through? Have you done much deep woods trekking, young lady?"

"No."

"No. Well, there's one thing you need to know, getting lost is easy. It's one of the easiest things a person can ever do. One might say we're lost most of the time anyway. How did you end up here? How did I? You go into the woods, and you might never come back."

"These woods are not that extensive, are they? It's not like I'm in the Cherokee National Forest. These woods probably don't cover more than, what? Fifty acres?"

"If you haven't been listening, let me say it plain. These woods ain't like any other woods you might have been in. Something is in there."

"What does that mean?"

"You saw the trailer park, right? Or what's left of it? These woods are taking it back. I can't say what's in these woods exactly, but something is. Look, I've been writing this history of the trailer park, and you know what I've discovered? It's the history of a fall."

"A fall."

"Yes. They built this place, I think, with an eye to growth. They wanted to expand the place northward."

He pointed off into the woods.

"But there's been no expansion. There never will be. This place gets smaller. It's been getting smaller since they opened it. It's like entropy, you see."

"Heat death."

"Yep, that's the ticket. This place is shrinking. Fewer trailers, fewer people. I expect soon to be the last one out here."

"Well, there's still two other people living here. You're not completely alone."

"Mr. Robinson told me yesterday that he's having his trailer hauled out of here at the end of the week and put down on his daughter's property out somewhere west of town. That'll leave me and Bertie Samson, and I don't expect her to last long. She's too old to live alone much longer."

"But one can hardly blame these woods for making people old."

"Don't blame the woods for that. Time's a hard taskmaster, and it loves these trees more than us. I'm just saying that these woods are surely taking back what's theirs faster than we can die off. Look at them old pallets. Do you see how the littlest twig can but open that concrete? Look right there. That ain't no giant root pushing through. That's a tendril what you could break off with two fingers. But you couldn't break that concrete with two fingers. You'd need a sledgehammer and, frankly, some bigger arms than mine to swing it with. Explain that if you can."

"I can't."

"I know you can't. Listen, young lady. Don't go off in them woods. Don't go off by yourself and don't go with anybody else for that matter. Please. These woods were here before any kind of folks and it'll be here when we're gone. They're like rocks. You couldn't get rid of them if you tried with all your might. But I suspect they might be getting rid of us."

Leah thanked Mr. Patchett and said she'd been glad to meet him, that she'd like to come back and maybe read some of his history of the trailer park. He said he'd be ever so glad to see her again and he'd keep a cold co-cola in the box for her. She turned away and strode down the dusty Road of Remembrance and made a mental note to bring him something sweet when she came back.

*****

There were only two weeks left before the semester started. Although Leah still hadn't gotten all the boxes in her apartment emptied, she wanted to go check out the Old Grey Cemetery before school started.

She had spent her grant money visiting places out of the country: Mexico, Japan, and the Czech Republic. But her plans had always included looking for lesser-known evil places here in the states. Internet searches on possible sites had yielded a strange find.

Larry Summers was an arrowhead collector; or, better said, he was an arrowhead finder and vendor. His webpage was stocked with pictures of his finds. There were scores of them. Most were ordinary, but some were of incredible beauty. Larry was coy about how and where he hunted for and found his treasures, but in one instance he had used the words "evil place" in discussing his searches. Leah had emailed him and told him about her project. He was intrigued and said that if she were ever in east Tennessee, she should give him a call, and he'd hook her up.

Hook me up? Is it a coincidence that I'm now in east Tennessee?

She called the number Larry had sent her and they agreed to meet at a Starbucks near the campus. To her surprise, Larry turned out to be much younger than she imagined. Watching him shuffle into the place and drop into a chair across from her, she guessed he couldn't be more than nineteen or twenty. Sun browned and tow headed, he wore a denim shirt washed to nearly white, khaki pants, and combat boots. He dropped a worn backpack onto the table and looked around the place.

"I've never been in a Starbucks before."

He was grinning like a possum.

"You're kidding."

"You know what. I'm gonna go wash my hands."

She just assumed "wash my hands" was a euphemism for peeing, but when he came out of the men's room, he was shaking water off his hands. He walked by the counter and grabbed a handful of paper napkins and set to drying his hands.

When he sat down again, he leaned over the table and extended his hand.

"Larry Summers, treasure finder. And you're Leah Grove. Demon hunter."

She laughed and said, "You have to go up to the counter and order. They don't have waiters."

"How gauche," he said and raised his pinkie in the air.

They drank coffee and she told him about her project. Larry was so disarming that she found herself telling him about lying to the committee and all the trouble that had followed. How she'd lost her Harvard position and went on the run, so to speak, ending up at the University of Tennessee.

"You're kinda young to have gotten into so much trouble so quick. Though it seems to me you've made a pretty soft landing. University of Tennessee. It's not like you're working at, I don't know, Starbucks?"

Leah nodded.

"You're not wrong. I guess I'm overly dramatic. Though I haven't mentioned how I screwed up my love life in the process. I mean, I've got more stuff going on too. Not just my academic fraud."

"I hear you."

"What about you? How'd you end up hawking arrowheads on the internet?"

"'Hawking'. That's rich. I gotta remember that. Maps. It all started with maps. I just love 'em. I can't remember when I didn't. I was about six or seven when my father bought a car and when he cleaned out the old one, he dropped a AAA road map on the driveway with all the other junk he was going to chuck out. He said I could have it—well, and that was that. Oh, and the first time I saw a topographic map! Forget about it. Looked at maps, bought maps, stole maps... I drew maps of my house, my neighborhood, and school. Geologic maps...weather maps... Man, hooked is what I was. You know, people have been making maps for thousands of years. There's a picture on the internet of a map on a clay tablet from Mesopotamia. Shoot, the very first map was probably somebody scratching a diagram with their finger in the dirt."

"Did you study cartography in school?"

"Nah, I dropped out of school."

"Where were you going?"

"Nowhere. I mean, I dropped out of high school, not college."

"Oh. Wow."

"Yeah, I can feel the 'twitch upon the thread' in your tone."

"I'm sorry. Is that a literary reference? Wait, don't tell me."

"Yeah, it's Waugh."

"*Brideshead*. I said don't tell me."

"My mother is an English teacher at the Pellissippi Community College. My dad teaches math there too."

"I don't guess they were thrilled with your decision."

"To drop out? I don't know. My brother went on and became a cardiologist, so there's that. They never hassled me much about it. Since I moved out of the house right after, they never got much of a chance."

"Do you still talk to them?"

"Of course. I eat dinner with them most Sunday nights. Everything's cool. My mother still gives me reading. I get a book a month."

"Waugh."

"And Faulkner. And Updike. And et cetera."

"So how did you get from maps to arrowheads?"

"So, I was up at the Historical Society looking at old maps, when I found some that detailed where Indian tribes had lived."

"Native American."

"Stand down, professor."

"Sorry."

"I laid those old maps over newer ones to try to find these places. I spent a whole winter driving around Tennessee and north Georgia looking for such paradises that weren't paved over and parking lotted. I found about twenty places where the old settlements were on farmland. And it occurred to me that when they plowed that land up come spring, they were likely to turn up artifacts from those old settlements."

"Including arrowheads."

"Bingo. Most of the farmers were happy enough to let me walk around in their plowed fields. It took three years to cover all the fields I found. Took another year of sneaking into fields where I didn't have permission. Last year I went down to the Mississippi delta area and came back with a buttload of new stuff. Pardon my French."

"So, tell me about the cemetery."

"So, I had found a Cherokee settlement on this old farmer's land. I went up to the house. The field had just been plowed. It was perfect. This old fella musta been a million years old. No, seriously, I guarantee he was a confederate soldier in some Tennessee regiment. Anywho, he wants to talk, you know. He's living alone. You know how it is. I'm glad to talk to him since he's giving me permission to scavenge his field. Eventually he gets around to talking about the Grey place, the cemetery and all. Tells me some of the history of the family. Claims to be distantly related to the Grey guy who built it—"

"Thomas Grey."

"Right. This old boy had a lot to say on a variety of subjects. I got there around ten and about noon he fed me part of his lunch and never stopped talking the whole time. It was deep into the afternoon when I was finally able to shake loose from him."

"It was nice of you to give him your time."

"What have I got but time? I was intrigued by the notion of the old cemetery and since it was a little late to start looking for artifacts, I decided to walk across the field and into those woods he'd pointed out to me. But I didn't make it to the cemetery or the old house which he swore was still standing."

"Why not?"

"Dude, I got sick."

"What do you mean?"

"I mean, I got dizzy, nauseated, bone-tired, and sweaty. It was like the Covid fell outta those oaks and covered me like a blanket."

"Wow."

"I've took sick fast before. Honestly, I didn't think too much of it. I had just caught a glimpse of some standing stones through the trees, which I assumed was the cemetery, but by then I'd lost interest. I just wanted to get home and get some aspirin and hit the bed."

"Can't blame you."

"Except, of course, the instant I stepped out of the woods and crossed the road into the field, I was a hundred percent better. That's when I knew that place was all kinds of wrong."

"Maybe you had an allergic reaction to something in the woods."

"Yeah, no. C'mon, demon hunter. The place was bad. It was a bad place. An evil place. You know all about that shit. Don't try and diminish what I'm telling you here."

"No. Not trying to do that. Just a protocol of mine, you know, look for a natural explanation first."

"Lemme ask you this. Did you go to that suicide forest in Japan?"

"That I did. I did indeed."

"Did you even for a minute consider a natural explanation for it?"

"I did not."

"Yeah. Well, you can take my word for it. Something ain't right at the Old Grey Cemetery."

"Okay. I guess I'm making a trip out there."

Larry leaned back. His coffee was gone. He was good-looking in an outdoorsy way, trim, and hard-looking. She really liked the scar that ran from the corner of his right eye down to the corner of his mouth.

"Maybe I could buy you dinner tonight. You know, for giving me your time like this."

She smiled. She also wondered what the hell she was doing. Yeah, he was nice looking. His body was rock hard, and his smile—well, she could easily imagine kissing him.

Wait. What? What in the world are you thinking?

He cocked his head and gave her a look.

"Let me tell you about my life, Professor Demonology. I don't have a house. Or an apartment. Or a trailer. I live outside. In a tent. Sometimes I sleep in the bed of my pickup. I shower, when I do shower, at truck stops on I-75. I live mostly on fast food and convenience store fare. You're a beautiful woman. Smart. Going places. You got no business with the likes of me."

She blushed.

"Can I give you some money. For your time?"

"Oh, demon girl, demon girl. I don't live like this cause I'm poor. I make a pretty good living selling stuff on the webs. This is just who I am. I'm an outside boy. I'm an eating beans out of the can type, and you ain't no sleeping bag girl. Listen, somewhere out there's a rich man who's looking for you. A professor's husband in the making. Take my advice and let him find you."

*****

After about twenty-five miles on Highway 33, rising steadily through the beech and blackgum trees, the beauty berry, and the beebalms, browning now in the burning autumn of east Tennessee, Leah turned onto a dirt road marked Grey Boulevard. *A dirt boulevard,* she thought. What's next? A cobble-stone interstate? One side of the road was blasted corn fields, bent and browned stubble, and on the other side was dense forest, green and black, dark, and deep. It looked untouched since the beginning of time.

Her GPS had stopped working when she turned onto Grey Boulevard. She had no signal. No matter. The Old Grey Cemetery had not appeared on any internet map. She had found it in a thick, dusty file of crumbling early Tennessee maps in the library at Yale.

So, she had gotten as far as the road, but now she was guideless. The cemetery probably hadn't been in use in a hundred years or more. Would there still be a road or path leading off this road to it?

The Grey Cemetery was named for—and built by—Thomas Grey, a gentleman farmer at a time when Tennessee likely had only one other man who could claim that title. From 1743 until his death in 1765, Grey ran his plantation in the style of an English farm as best he could, despite his modest means. For the first eighteen years, he labored as hard as any of the enslaved people or free workers under his command. Over time, fortune favored him: he grew wealthy, sent to Boston for a wife, became an early advocate for Tennessee statehood, and raised four children. Yet, as soon as they reached adulthood, all four left for the Northeast—and never returned, except to be laid to rest.

Leah had left before light. Now the sun was a flame-white disk just above the mountains in the east and fog lay on the ground billowing like silk sheets. To the west storm clouds loomed.

She followed a long curve that descended slowly, and she came to a fork. The right hand was less traveled. *I can't remember now. Wasn't there some controversy about the poem, whether the less-traveled road was better or not?* In truth, neither looked like it had been driven on in some time. She took the one that appeared more traveled.

The road petered out into a clearing. She thought maybe she had come upon the cemetery after all, so she got out and walked around looking for stones. What she found were the ruins of a house. Obviously, the great house of the Grey family, a wandering brick edifice climbed over by vines and kudzu. She walked around for a while and found the outlines of two smaller buildings, kitchen probably and maybe a storage building. She got back in the car and turned around. But then she got out and climbed on the roof and looked into the distances in every direction. *Where would I have put the cemetery, were I old Thomas?*

The land seemed to fall off to the west. That's where the road not taken went! It would only make sense to put the graveyard lower than the house and its well. Same theory with an outhouse.

She headed back to the fork and went east.

The road was tougher. In fact, it was less road and more just her following a vehicle sized path through the trees. Limbs and bushes scraped the doors and windows. The ground continued to fall. At one point the path was so steep that she thought she might be driving off the side of a mountain. The road, the path or whatever, was just about done.

I might as well throw it in reverse and back outta here, she thought.

And then—there was a huge boulder blocking her way forward. She pushed her door open and climbed out through the bushes pressed up against her car. The rock was mammoth. Twice as tall as her, like something out of the Rocky Mountains, gray with streaks of rust, it stood there as ridiculously out of place as Wallace Steven's jar, also from Tennessee. The morning was cool, and the mist drifted from behind the rock around her ankles. She touched it. It was warm. She looked up through the trees. No sign of the sun. She laid her cheek on the surface of the boulder and closed her eyes. Warm, almost hot.

She was suddenly shaky and too warm, her mind filled with confusing and irrelevant thoughts: bad choices, people she'd hurt, mistakes with money, the bad decisions she'd made in her short life falling like leaves, like conjuring cards all face up on the ground around her.

Gray and black clouds pushed farther east, blocking the sun.

She sat on the ground and leaned back against a tree. She pressed her hands to her face, and they felt cool, and she could feel the bark of the tree through her jacket and shirt. After a minute she felt more grounded, more in control. What a been a faint background drone of cicadas rose now, louder and louder until she began to doubt whether the sound could be real or not.

Leah took a few deep breaths and got to her feet. She felt a little better, but she was torn. The greatest part of her was calling her to get back in her car and get out of here. She looked at the boulder and her head felt light, and she thought she might have to sit down again. She looked at the car. She wanted to get in it. The trees around her seemed to want her to get in it. The car itself seemed to call to her. The air buzzed with the sawing of the cicadas.

She turned away from the car and the boulder and walked off into the trees away from both.

After a hundred yards or so of trees, she saw the cemetery. A wrought-iron fence with a fallen gate, weeds as tall as the stones and markers. No mausoleum. Disappointing.

She pushed through the weedy ground to the tallest stone: Thomas Grey. Okay. Well, there it is. *Father, Husband, Patriot.*

The air was yellow. The sky black and the air yellow. Storm coming. Bad storm. Tiny pieces of ice, the size of watermelon seeds fell sideways.

She sat on the other side of old Tom's headstone and wished for her hoodie. The temperature had dropped, and it was suddenly as cold as January. *Father, Husband, Patriot.* She tried to make herself small against the hail.

If this was an evil place, she couldn't feel it. She had always relied on feelings. And history. Not that she didn't feel something. What she felt, now, here in the abandoned and forgotten burial grounds of the Grey family was doubt. That familiar nagging specter that questioned every choice she made. That made her doubt her intellect, education and her very common sense.

And what will your epitaph read? Who will raise your stone? What child, what mate?

The ice fall stopped, and she got up and headed back toward her car. She had a moment's hesitation at the cemetery gate. She'd come out of the woods at a right angle to the fence.

Isn't that right?

She stepped off into the woods. Even among the trees the wind was formidable. A limb dropped loudly to her left and she looked up. The sky was a sickening yellow, indicative of the worst kind of storm.

She couldn't find the car. When she stepped out of the trees into a clearing and saw the Grey house, she understood that she had, somehow and against all reason, missed her car altogether.

How did I walk this far?

She felt dizzy again. Her head was spinning, and she wanted more than anything to lie down. She turned toward the house. She couldn't go inside. Surely the thing would collapse on top of her.

She sat on the edge of the porch. The wood was soft and papery. She was nauseated and her head was throbbing. A black blob was growing in the center of her vision. What she needed to do was take some pictures, but she'd foolishly left her camera in the car.

How do you get out of the car without the camera? I mean, that's what you came here for.

She needed to find her car and get her camera. Do what she came here to do.

She stood up and walked away from the house. Her nausea tapered off some and she could see better the farther she got from the house. Her legs felt weak though, and she sat down abruptly in the weedy yard. She could feel the house behind her. In the sky the clouds were rushing toward the east and the yellow cast of the light deepened. She was in a headachy sepia photograph.

Above the deafening chorus of cicadas, a new sound rose— a distant roar. A train? An avalanche? Neither made sense. Then she saw it: an oak tree, wrenched from the earth as if by invisible hands, soaring skyward like a missile before slamming back to the ground. Her breath caught. Tornado.

The trees around her hid the horizon, but the swirling cloud of debris left no doubt. Panic surged through her veins as she scanned her surroundings. The house loomed nearby, but it was no refuge—not against this. She needed shelter, something low, solid. Or better yet... her car.

She ran into the trees trying to retrace her steps. Then she saw the boulder. *Is that thing bigger?* Despite the fact that she'd squeezed by it before, now it was jammed between two trees.

Her car was on the other side of it. At least that's where she'd left it.

Please let it be there. She kicked through the brush on the other side of one of the trees and got around the boulder.

Her car wasn't there.

And you knew it wasn't going to be here, didn't you? Now what?

The path she'd driven on was there, so she started running toward the dirt road she'd turned off of to get here. Flying leaves, pine needles, and dirt were hitting her. There were no tracks from her tires, either on the path or on the dirt road.

So where is my freaking car?

She ran down the dirt road until she was out of the woods. The fallow corn fields were to her left and out there about two hundred yards into a soggy-looking field sat her car.

How in the world?

Beyond that, the tornado was twisting and jumping across the field, basically heading right for the car.

Leah decided to make a run for it. Get in the car and get out of the way of that freaking monster. Just before she started running, she heard her grandmother's voice, soft, urgent, flowing under the noise of noisy leaves. One word: *no.*

She turned around and ran back through the trees toward the house.

Any port in a storm, as they say.

She came out in the graveyard. She ran between the gravestones toward what she assumed would be the house, but suddenly she was falling and hit the ground hard enough to knock the wind out of her.

And no wonder. She looked around and understood she had fallen into an open grave.

There had been no open grave before. Why in the world would there be an open grave out here, in a cemetery that hadn't been used in over a century?

Leah had hurt her wrist in the fall, and her knee was aching. She stood and reached for the edge of the grave. She could get her hand over the edge but there was nothing to grab hold of to pull herself up. The tornado sounded for all the world like a train running right over her head. Then it got dark.

She was in nightmare territory.

She felt the walls of the grave, hoping to find something that would give her some purchase with which to pull herself up and out. There was a great whooshing and a giant tree fell across the opening of the grave. She threw herself to the ground and crawled into a corner.

Is this where it all ends? Has my story reached its inevitable denouement?

And just as quickly, the storm was over. The train roar of the tornado was gone. The sky lightened, the wind dropped. How was she going to get out of this grave? *This grave that wasn't here ten minutes ago.* She could climb out through the branches of the tree that had fallen over the opening, if she could somehow reach them. She tried to jump up and grab a branch but couldn't quite reach.

I need a ladder.

But she didn't. In a quick minute she realized she could dig out footholds in the side of the grave. It took a while. Her hands got very tired and there was enough dirt under her nails to start a tomato garden, but she eventually reached the tree and climbed out through the limbs.

Standing next to the tree covered grave, she took stock. Leah was muddied beyond recognition and bone-tired with a sore knee and wrist. Well, at least she hadn't been chucked up into the sky toward Oz. She cut out through the trees and walked into the field where her car was.

So, either I left the car out in the field—though why I'd do that, I have no idea—or the tornado picked it up and dropped it here. Upright. Completely undamaged. Yeah... you might be losing it, demon girl.

She got her camera and went back for pictures of the house and cemetery. She was light-headed, but nothing like the nausea and dizziness from before.

And yet, she'd heard Effie's voice as clear as a bell. Just one word. But definitely Effie.

Girl, it's time to get her outta that home.

*****

Leah stared at her phone. At the number to the nursing home where Effie lived. She had planned to wait until she was more settled, tenured maybe, certainly in her own house, before she moved Effie in with her. Now, tenure seemed like a long way away, maybe even a pipedream. She was probably going to end up as a low paid instructor right here in Tennessee for the rest of her career. Her meeting with Mr. Patchett reminded her that Effie was not going to live forever.

You don't even know if she'll want to come.

She touched the number, and it started ringing way out there in Oklahoma.

Eventually, Effie came to the phone.

"Effie. Can you hear me?"

"Like you were standing right next to me, sweetheart. It's so good to hear your voice."

"I don't call enough, I know. I'm a terrible granddaughter, but I've kinda finished my traveling and have taken root here in Tennessee. Knoxville."

"That's nice."

"Look. I'm teaching at the college here, and I'm only living in an apartment, but I want you to come and stay with me now. For good."

"That's a lot of trouble for you, I think."

"It ain't no trouble for me, Effie."

"'Ain't no'? Is that the kinda talk you done learnt up there to the Yale College?

"'Done learnt?' 'Up to the Yale College?' You're mocking me? We're on the phone less than a minute and you're mocking me already? How am I gonna put up with you for two days in the car?"

"It is a nice time of year for a car ride."

"Well, I can stand it if'n you can."

"'If'n' I can'. Lordy, girl. The way you talk. And you with that doctoral degree in English."

"My degree is in Religion. Comparative Religion."

"I don't s'pose it keeps you outta much in the way of sin though."

"Have mercy."

"And I don't know how you're gonna find a man dragging some old blind woman around behind you," Effie said.

"What makes you think I'm looking for a man?"

"A girl then. I don't care. But you need somebody."

"Effie, for Pete's sake. Will you climb up off'n my back now?"

"'Off'n'."

"Fine. You win. But what I want is for you to come over here and live with me now. I miss you. I've missed you so much. I've wasted so much time with this whole education thing. I'm not sure it was worth it. Anyway, we're a package deal. If the man I choose can't take you, then I don't want him."

"Or her."

Leah said, "Good grief. Maybe I deserve this acid tongue of yours. It's true that I haven't been the best person of late."

"Okay then. Come get me."

"You beat all, Effie. Okay. I'm driving out there right away. Pack your toothbrush and your nightie and whatever else you have. If I leave in the morning, I'll be there by Wednesday. Will you be ready?"

"It'll take me all of five minutes to pack."

"So, you tell whoever runs that place that you're outta there come Wednesday, okay?"

"Okay."

The next morning Leah loaded the car. The nursing home was a good nine-hundred-miles away, two days of all day driving.

At least. You have probably overestimated your driving skills.

She packed a cooler with some juice boxes and sandwiches and got into her traveling clothes, basically sleep pants and an extra-large tee shirt.

The one useful lesson she'd learned in her travels was that books on tape make the time pass so much more quickly than staring out the window. For her trip she'd gotten three Alice Hoffman books: *Seventh Heaven*, *Practical Magic*, and

Blackbird House. She loved Hoffman's books, the taste of her sentences, the quirky women out of step with the world, the way that the unseen kept crossing into the actual. Actual good and evil forces in characters' lives.

During the afternoon, on a long flat stretch of empty interstate, Leah saw some farmers burning fields north of the highway. She turned off the book tape. The tingly smell of the fires was seeping into the car even though the windows were closed. Taste and smell. Ah, the great mnemonics.

She remembered the thirteenth year of her life as the first year of her life in the orphanage.

The young girl is having the drowning dream again. All around her in the dark, sleeping orphans twitch, snore, whimper, cry. The building is a former Army barracks, and Leah imagines the bunks the children sleep in once bore the tired bodies of soldiers, holy boys bound for war, and that the former sleepers in these beds, all dead now, killed in war or killed by time, sometimes stand ghostly next to the bunks at night and watch the girls in their sleep.

In her dream, Leah has always swum down too deep and is now unable to reach the surface before her lungs suck in water all by themselves, will she or nil she. Still yards from the surface, she breathes in deeply but somehow doesn't drown. She never drowns, but tonight? The air she breathes is smoky, like a campfire or a fireplace. She breathes in, it seems, whole wet smoky blankets.

She wakes coughing. The room is full of smoke and very hot. Girls scream and cry and run amok in the thick smoldering darkness. Leah rolls out of the bunk and crawls to the window. When she pushes it open, a cold wind rushes past her into the building and the room behind her explodes. She is thrown outside onto the hard dirt of the playground. She isn't hurt badly. The building is now fully engulfed in fire.

She sprints to the front door and yanks it open. The handle is so hot it scalds the skin off her palm. Nobody. All the bunks are burning. The ceiling is on fire. The second story must be like the inside of a kiln or blacksmith oven. The floor down here isn't burning, so she covers her mouth and starts looking for girls.

The air is full of floating fire, fragments of nightgowns, pages of picture books, strands of hair, floating, burning.

No one lying between the bunks. She feels her way to the back. The girls are pressed against the back door, locked as it always was with a key only Mrs. Bolton had.

Above the roaring voice of the fire, she hears someone sobbing, calling for help. The sound is coming from beneath the pile of dead girls before her.

Hello, she shouts.

Behind her a beam falls across the room, a braid of flames that knocks burning bunks into one another like hellish dominoes. She takes a dead girl by the arm and drags her out into the burning room. The next girl is one she knows well—Diane Harper. Her face is gray, smudged, serene. She pulls Diane by the feet off the pile. Girl after girl after girl, all in some way known to her in greater and lesser degree. All dead.

Finally, she sees an arm waving, and she pulls the girl out of the pile and drags her across the burning room, jumping over the burning beam, and toward the door, through the door, outlined in flames, and out into the night, the clear air, the cool air, the hard stars in the dark firmament of the sky. She lies on her back and deciphers from the tracks of the wandering stars the journey that awaits her, beyond this burning building, beyond the whirr of cicadas, the whisper of smoke, the roar of machines, the hysterical voices, the pulling hands, the close faces, the stricken looks on the faces....

She wakes in the hospital. There is no good news. Only she has survived. There is something wrong, she thinks, with the lights. They shimmer, they hum, and she hears under the hum something like the sound of voices. Pastel angels wipe her brow, whisper encouragement. Doctors in white, so white she squints. They say things. They smile and write on clipboards and go away.

When she left the hospital, the Children Services people placed her into an orphanage in another county. The accommodations there were nicer than the abandoned barracks. The food was better, she thought. She shared a room with only two other girls, which was nice. The girls were shy and circumspect, and they kept their distance because, it turned out, she was something of a celebrity. The other children at the new orphanage had heard the story of the fire, of her miraculous escape, and they held her to be something of a talisman, a good luck charm. Boys kissed her wrists and the girls asked to smell her hair. They said they could still smell smoke in it, though Leah couldn't. Whenever prospective parents came to the facility, every child ran their fingers across the door to her room and—if they could find her—touched her on her bare skin for luck.

Leah had no such luck. At least none to give herself. She could rub her own door and kiss her own wrists and smell her smoky hair as much as she liked: nobody was going to adopt her.

Looking back, Leah knew that she hadn't done much to help her chances. When those sad, hopeful couples came looking for a child, that special child who would fill the quiet halls of their homes and light the dark corners of their rooms, the child who would complete their lives, Leah would ask them weird questions, questions that even now she could not fathom the origin of.

Did you ever forgive him? What do you think that baby is like now? Did your husband ever find out?

And the counselors would remind her, *don't talk, Leah, just don't say anything, and especially don't say these random things, or no one will ever adopt you.*

Even now, she could feel the same urgency that had once driven her to ask questions—an instinctive sense that her life somehow depended on the answers. It was as though she lived inside an existential matrix where every decision, every choice, irrevocably sealed off countless possibilities or, just as easily, opened vast chasms beneath her feet from which there was no return, all in the awful daring of a single moment.

She had been the girl whose intuition and presence unsettled everyone around her—so much so that, once she was grown, they allowed her to leave home. And when she did, she stopped asking questions. She tried to bury those unsettling parts of herself, to make them invisible.

For her, the world was a numinous, living thing—a firefly world glowing in a soft blue night, alive with velvety darkness and twinkling lights. This awareness helped her realize that she possessed a deep sensitivity to place, an intuition that had drawn her into the study of sacred spaces in the first place.

She knew it was true. On the rare occasions she visited these revered sites, she felt their sacredness far more intensely than those around her. The experience was beyond belief. Yet she also discovered holiness in unexpected places—at lonely roadsides where a single oak tree stood surrounded by bare earth, the grass long killed by tire tracks. Still, people came. They were drawn there by something she could feel in the depths of her heart.

Why that tree? Other trees lined the road, other views were just as beautiful and compelling, and yet this was the one that called people to it. Some force beyond understanding pulled them there.

And yet she wondered: what was it that called to *her*—that called to Leah herself—not just to places of awe and wonder, where the presence of God or gods could be felt, but to the darkness? What drew her toward the things and places that frightened her, toward those that glowed with the unsettling light of evil?

Was it some sort of vengeance thing over her parents?

She left the orphanage when she came of age. Before she finished high school.

And so she was forced to construct herself in such a fashion that the world would be able to accept her. In the orphanage and in the time after, she had confronted the mirror, the one that gave her back the face she wanted to show the world. And the face she wanted to hide. She built a fortress around herself. She styled her hair like a pre-Raphaelite Venus, affected loose blouses and leggy pants and flowing scarves. Wore rings on every finger. Smiled. And she wove little nests of sentences and judgments and beliefs to stand in her place. She constructed herself, waiting tables, studying for her GED on lunch breaks, dinner breaks, late shifts. She was the girl who did that.

Not for the first time, she felt certain she had lived in other eras—that she had been reincarnated. Whether that sensation came from the stories her father once read to her, from things she had heard even before she was born, or from her own imaginings as a child growing up in orphanages, she could not say. But she sensed a pattern in her life, a mythic journey unfolding before her, as if it had been mapped long ago—before history itself.

It was as though she had been called out of the ordinary world, a world that was never truly her home, and summoned to cross a threshold into another realm. There, she would meet allies and adversaries, face ordeals, and enter a crucible that would refine her in fire and light.

She went to Yale and wrote that dissertation—all that work, little more than a misstep, the wrong path chosen. Her professors were so sure and that made her sure, sure that wherever she was going was somewhere out there beyond her investigation and study of sacred places. Out beyond the book she would write and the jobs she would try on before tenuring in somewhere. But sacred places would not be her trial, her ordeal. She took their money with every intention of following through, with every intention of meeting the destiny her committee foresaw for her. But that had not come to pass. She had abandoned her plans to study the holy and sacred sites so precious to the Religion Department.

Instead, she had sought out dark places—deliberately, purposefully—not to see what she could learn, but to discover what she could *feel*. She knew, as surely as she knew anything, that a curtain exists all around us: invisible yet ever-present, swaying just beyond perception. And what she wanted, more than anything, was to part that veil—the unseen barrier that separates us from Good and Evil, but mostly... from Evil.

It all went wrong just before she left on the first leg of her journey. She was meeting with her committee for the last time before she left. There was some exchange of paperwork, handshakes all around, lots of clapping on one another's back. Everyone was very pleased with themselves, not least of all her. As the meeting broke up, Professor Schwarz pulled her aside and gave her a copy of the list of holy sites she planned visit over the next year or so. On them he had scratched out Stonehenge and penciled in Teotihuacán.

She stared at the paper.

"Teoti—what?"

"Teotihuacán. The Pyramid of the Sun, about fifty clicks north of Mexico City. It's an Aztec temple."

"Aztec. Really?"

"Holiness comes in many forms, Miss Grove," and with that, he left the room.

She thought it more than just a little late in the process to be making such big adjustments in the grant proposal, but he was who he was and there was no getting around that.

I'll tell you what, old son. I am going to Stonehenge if I have to hitchhike and sleep on the ground. What the hell?

She visited a couple of places in Central America, but knew she had to go to Teotihuacán whether she wanted to or not. The Pyramid of the Sun. But when she got there and saw the thing, everything changed. Why in the world had Schwartz sent her here? This was no holy place. Hundreds of victims had been dragged up those steps and dispatched with a bloody stone knife. What's holy about that?

More to the point, evil radiated off the place like deadly uranium protons off an exposed nuclear rod.

The tourists moved around her like a stream around a boulder. They couldn't wait to get near it, to climb it, to put their hands on the centuries-old blood-soaked stone. She tried to move forward. The air seemed thick beyond the natural humidity. The sky, misty and gray on the ride over, was dazzling blue and so bright it hurt her eyes.

She tried the first step. It was a block of stone three feet high. She was dizzy and headachy and swaying so badly that the local guards took her gently by the arms and led her away from the temple to a small lean-to and gave her a cold Ade.

Sitting in the shade, sticky with sweat, sick to her stomach, she fell into a waking dream. Up from the dust raised by the tourists' flip flops and sandals, images of feathered headdresses, burning eyes, dripping knives, red-eyed, blue-robed priests spilling the blood of jaguars and virgin daughters with obsidian blades for their black-hearted gods.

She passed out and woke in the lobby of her hotel. A man was holding her wrist.

"Miss Grove? Ah, good. Can you hear me? Yes? I'm Dr. Gasset. I'm afraid you have a little heat exhaustion, and you're dehydrated. But you're going to be all right."

"Aztec," she whispered.

"Yes, of course. I'm not putting you in the hospital. I believe you just need some rest and a lot of water. I want you to go to your room now and go to bed. Sleep as much as you can. Drink water every time you wake up all night. And stay in the hotel tomorrow. No sun. Okay?"

The next day she felt fine. She went back to the temple, but she kept her distance. She took pictures and talked to the people who worked there. She stayed there all day. She spent a lot of time wondering why in the world Professor Schwarz had sent her here. Yes, the murderous, bloody ceremonies of the Aztecs were religious. They were attempts at appeasement of their gods. But—holy? Had she misunderstood what the word *holy* meant?

Her understanding of holy places had been centered on those instances when ordinary profane space became sacred space. When the divine broke through into the ordinary world and changed people and places. She had visited Talpa de Allende before she came to Teotihuacán. It had been a perfect place to include in the book she was writing. A Christian site built on top of a place dedicated to the worship of the pagan Earth Goddess Cohuacoatl. What could be better?

She took pictures. She talked to locals. She felt nothing.

But Teotihuacán changed everything.

In the late afternoon she sat in the shadow of the pyramid and came to a decision.

She couldn't do the project. She had taken the university's money, but she could no longer see herself doing the work. She had completely lost interest in holy sites. Holy sites were real enough. She'd spoken to enough people to know that. She, on

94

the other hand, couldn't feel it. She couldn't feel the sacred in those places.

But she could feel evil.

At least, she assumed that was what she was feeling. But she *was* feeling something. She couldn't imagine spending the next few years visiting places like Lourdes and Stonehenge, then another year writing about them—only to feel nothing. She didn't want her work to leave her numb. She needed fire, a reason to keep going. The Good felt tepid. Evil burned.

Was it that simple? Satan is more exciting than God. The whole *Paradise Lost* thing? Really?

She had the university's money. She wasn't giving it back. She was going to the evil places, but she needed to talk to someone. Timothy was out. He didn't even believe in God, much less Good and Evil. Quentin. Pointless. She could call Elizabeth who would talk her out of it. Effie would be best, but she would never approve of taking the committee's money and then running off with it to do whatever she wanted.

So, she called Jack Barry. He was the oldest member of her committee, a New Testament scholar and translator of Gnostic gospels. She told him about the temple and what she'd experienced and what she was going to do. He did not sound completely shocked, but he tried to talk her out it. He told her that no one at the university would understand.

"They will be royally pissed off. You must know that, right?"

"Maybe if I write a good book, they'll understand?"

"I'm sure you will write a good book. And I'm sure they'll understand. But I am also sure that what they will *not* do is forgive you. They won't take you back here. You'll be finished here at Yale."

This drew her up short. It took her breath away.

She said, "There are other places to teach. If my book's good, somebody will hire me."

"Well, as long as you don't need too many recommendations," he said.

"I can't help it. My heart's no longer in the other. I have to do this."

"Okay then." Dr. Berry took a deep breath. "Consider this at least. Maybe this is not a good path to take. What do you think is going to happen to you, visiting all these evil places?"

"I don't know what you mean. What could happen to me?"

"Why do you think people are drawn to sacred places, what do you think they want?"

She said, "They want to encounter the numinous, they want to be closer to their god or gods, and they want the feelings of the divine, and they hope that their gods will become close to them."

"And if you go to these evil places you've mapped out, regardless of what you want, regardless of your intentions, what is it that you're seeking? Have you considered that the very evil you seek may attach itself to you? You know? Nietzsche? The Abyss? Something staring back at you?"

"I'm sorry," she said, "you sound like a science fiction novel."

"I'm sure you must mean a horror novel," he said. "Do you think you are the first to come up with this idea? You're not that unique, Leah. What do you think happened to them? They're dead."

Then he listed off five cases of scholars who died under mysterious circumstances while looking into the phenomenon of evil places.

"And maybe," he said, "maybe you just don't tempt fate."

After they hung up, those names rang in her ears.

*****

She stopped in Forrest City, Arkansas, for the night, but was up and out before daylight. She got to the Cedars of Lebanon Retirement Home around seven the next night. She hadn't thought it through very well. It was too late to put Effie into the car and hit the road. Effie said they should just stay the night in her room and leave the next morning. The lady running the home was super nice and said that would be fine and that they would miss Effie so much. Leah slept on the short sofa in Effie's room, and the next morning they had breakfast with the other residents of the home.

Leah decided on a more leisurely return trip. They would spread it out over three days instead of two. Leah didn't play the book on tape but told Effie about her apartment and the job she had at the university in Knoxville.

Effie asked if she had a boyfriend.

Leah hesitated before she said no.

"That was a long road to a 'no'," Effie said.

"What does that mean?"

"Oh. Sorry. It means I think you might be fibbing."

"'Fibbing'? What am I? Twelve?"

"No, I believe you're twenty-five, twenty-six years old? Isn't that right? About the right age to be having a steady boyfriend."

"Effie, I only got to Knoxville three weeks ago. I haven't even started working yet."

"Thinking you'll find something among the student body then?"

Leah sighed.

"You beat all, you know that."

"Maybe. But I was of the impression that you had somebody up at Yale College that you were sweet on."

"Really? And how did you get under that impression?"

"I *marked* it when you called me from there last year."

"You marked it, did you?"

"Yes or no, missy?"

"'Missy'? Well, I guess I'm put in my place all right."

Effie didn't say anything.

Leah got the feeling she was waiting on an answer, so she said, "I was seeing a boy, a man really, named Timothy."

"And did you like him?"

"Well, I was seeing him. Actually, I moved in with him for a little while."

"Without benefit of clergy?"

"Yes, Effie, without benefit of clergy. Who talks this way?"

"I'm just gathering the facts."

"It's the twenty-first century, you know."

"Only too well, darling. And so, did he finally put you out?"

"Put *me* out! No, I left him."

"I guess he shouldn't have been giving the milk away for free."

"Giving the—wow. Just wow."

"And so you left him. Why?"

"It's a long story."

"It's a long ride."

So, Leah told her the story of the debacle at Yale, the misspent grant money, Timothy and his rich family, the loss of her job, her search for another one, and ending up in Tennessee.

"I guess you think I'm a proper fool," Leah said.

"There are a couple of places in the story you might have made better decisions, but nobody lives a perfect life. What seems like a mistake at one place and time may look better from a vantage farther down the road."

"I guess."

"But that ain't all, is it?"

"What do you mean?"

Effie was quiet a moment.

Then she said, "The other fellow."

Now it was Leah's turn to be quiet. More than just a couple of miles went by in silence. Effie's face was turned toward the window, as if she might have been looking at the flashing scenery, which of course she wasn't.

"I'm not sure I want to talk about him."

"Ashamed?"

"Just a skosh."

"Go ahead."

"I wish I could tell you what I was really after."

"A way out?"

"Maybe. Probably. I don't know."

But Leah did know. She was teaching two classes, and she had just come back from Stull Cemetery in Kansas where she'd gone on spring break. She was overwhelmed by what she had seen. She wanted to—she needed to—go back in the coming summer so she could spend more time interviewing locals. But right then she had a problem. She was required to meet with her grant committee to give her report before the end of the semester. The problem was that she had no business being at

Stull Cemetery. She was either going to have to lie and say she went to Lourdes or something, or she was going to have to admit she went somewhere else. For an entirely different purpose than the one they were paying for.

Leah was hiding deep in the library stacks, considering her choices. Timothy was expecting her home soon. She didn't want to face the committee. Now she didn't want to face Timothy either. He'd been asking questions about her trip, and she'd been deflecting as hard as she could. He obviously knew something was wrong. He would expect her to explain herself to him. So would the committee. She had come to a fork in the road. And when you come to a fork in the road, you take it.

Then she saw him. The fork.

His long dark hair fell over his face. His face was dark with stubble. His clothes were dark, long black overcoat over black jacket and dark blue jeans. He dropped a book on the table across from her and fell into a chair. He flung the book open as if he were disgusted by it and hung his head over it, like he was praying. Somehow, she choked on her own spit and coughed loudly. He looked up.

"You okay, teach?"

Of course, his eyes were as dark as the rest of him. Common courtesy would have made him drop his eyes after a second, but he continued to stare at her long after courtesy had gotten up and left the room and caught the bus out of town.

It was Quentin. Leah got up and went to his table. She sat without invitation and started asking him questions. He was working on his master's degree in American Literature, but what he wanted to do was write his own poetry. His hands were not clean. There was a smudge of something on his face. She could smell him, wool and sweat. He was dead broke. He lived in two rooms in a basement in the poorest part of New Haven.

He was the anti-Timothy.

She drove him to his poor abode and spent the night with him.

*****

"I have a couple of questions," Effie said.

"Not shocked."

"Tell me about that trip you took on the grant money."

"Like what?"

"Suppose you'd done what you were supposed to? What would that have looked like?"

"Pictures of sacred places, narratives of their histories, such as that."

"And what you did instead?"

"Nothing publishable, that's for sure."

"Say what?"

"Fewer pictures, some history, good interviews, but way too much of my own phenomenological reactions to the place on a quantum slash spiritual level."

"Again, please, in English."

"I didn't write a scholarly book. I didn't write anything you could stack in the Yale library. It was, or will be, something more personal."

"And Yale doesn't countenance the personal."

"Not so much. I mean, I took pictures, I researched the history of the places, but what I really did was try to feel something."

"Okay."

"In the sacred places I wrote about for my dissertation, I thought I could feel something in those places, something compelling, something attractive, something calling to me. The numinous."

"Well, that's God, don't you think."

"Maybe. I certainly couldn't discount it. But I am not interested in that."

"In God."

"No. I mean the sacred places—how can I say this? Sometimes I got a feeling. Most times I didn't. I'm not sure any more about sacred places. Maybe they're sacred, maybe they're not. What I do know is that when I went to places that people call evil, I did feel something. I felt horror and terror and fear. I know, as sure as I know my name, that something is going on there. I can't say that about sacred places. Okay, so if the Uluru rock formation in Australia attracts people, makes them feel something, spirit or God or connected to the universe, fine. But I know that if I go there, I'm not going to feel anything like what I felt at Teotihuacán.

"You are one odd child, you know that?"

"Yes, I know that."

"So, tell me about the boy."

"The boy?"

"The one you left up in New England."

"That really is a tough one."

"You love him, don't you?"

The question caught her off guard. The easy answer should have been "no," but hearing Effie say it made something in her chest catch and her eyes brimmed.

"Lord, I'm sorry, child. I didn't mean to upset you."

Effie couldn't have seen her tears, or felt Leah's what? — Longing? Desire? Regret? —that seemed to be pushing its way out of her.

"Well," Leah said, wiping her tears, "He is beautiful."

"Beautiful? Like a woman?"

"Close to. If you could see his skin. Have mercy, his arms are so strong. I don't know. He could be on the cover of a romance novel."

"If you say so. But you didn't finally want him, was that it?"

"I did want him. I do want him. I know that now. I think I'm missing him for the first time today."

"You could call him."

"I don't know what I'd say."

"When you really love somebody, the words don't matter."

"It's more than that. I mean, I know he loves me. But honestly, I don't think he knows me. He likes me on the outside, the way I look, the way I talk, my sense of humor. Maybe. But see if this don't draw you up short...I'm pretty sure that he thought once I finished my Ph.D., I'd quit the university and be his wife full time."

"Would that be so bad?"

"Yep. Yes, it would. I've got skills. I got research skills. I can write. I can teach. And what? I'm going to quit all that so I can tell the maids when to polish the silver and what flowers to put out in the foyer?"

"Pardon me? Did you say maids? As in the plural? More than one maid?"

"Did I mention that his family has money? Lots of money?"

"You said they had money. I don't think you said lots."

"Well, they do. And that kind of pisses me off."

"Language."

"Okay. It irritates me all the way to aggravation."

"Better. Though I don't know how money can make you mad."

"Well, it does. It did. Not so much now, I don't guess. It's not his fault he's rich. You should have seen him trying to impress me when we first got together. Flowers, fancy dinners. And his car! It cost more than I make in two good years."

"A man uses what he can to get a woman he wants."

"I understand 'want.' I do. 'Wine comes in at the mouth, and love comes in at the eye'."

"That's nicely put."

"Yeah, I didn't make it up. When I first saw him, I wanted him. I wanted him to take me to bed. But that's all on the outside. I didn't know him. Truth be told, I assumed that's what he wanted. Just to take me to bed and be done with it."

"Men can be like that."

"And if that was what he wanted, well, he might just have gotten it."

"Meaning what?"

"Meaning maybe I got what I wanted too. Hit it and quit it."

"I know what that means. They say it on the television. So, what? You're a man now?"

"It sounds terrible, I know. But I might could have just used him for sex. Lots of girls do. But—I don't know. I got to feeling something for him. Something beyond just the sexual. I can't tell you what it was."

"Maybe it was love."

"Maybe. Could be. What does that feel like?"

"Probably something like standing in one of those cathedrals or rock formations you went to see."

"Something ineffable, I guess."
"Effable?" Effie said.

CHAPTER FIVE

Light does not come from light,
but from darkness.
~Mircea Eliade

Timothy rolled up his sleeves and looked around. His cubicle was in the virtual center of the room, which was full of cubicles. Something was wrong with the air conditioning, and it was hothouse humid. He'd abandoned his jacket and loosened his tie. Some of the older hands had pulled tiny battery-powered, hand-held fans out of their desks and were waving them before their shiny faces. Metropolitan Life and Casualty. His new employer.

Yes, he could have taken the job his friend Chris offered him or the one his college girlfriend Amanda had offered him. Both were virtual sinecures—jobs that paid well and had almost no responsibilities—but pride had made him turn them down. Politely. He had determined not to ask for help. He hadn't asked either Chris or Amanda.

Was it worse that they heard it on some New Haven grapevine that I was out at Lowell and Sons?

They just called him up and offered him work. He could do better than this. Hell, in six months he'd be promoted and have an office here and would be all these people's boss.

Of that he had no doubt.

But was that what he wanted?

In truth, nothing felt right anymore without her. Leah.

Amanda had hinted that her offer came with perks, that she was available, again. More than one woman here at Metropolitan had left her name and number on his desk while he was out at lunch. He couldn't get interested.

Does that mean I love her?

Timothy wiped his brow with a handkerchief. He'd rarely pulled his handkerchief out before. He carried it because his father carried one. Because his grandfather did. Because his mother asked him every time he left the house if he had one. He made a note in his phone to buy a battery-powered, hand-held fan. The phone rang.

It was the skip-tracer.

Timothy stood up and nodded at Roger Worth, the office manager, who nodded back, acknowledging that Timothy was taking a break. Timothy left the room and walked down the much cooler hallway toward the executive offices. In front of the elevators, he answered the call.

"Mr. Tompkins," Timothy said.

"Mr. Lowell. I have found your party."

"Excellent. Where is she?"

"Let's talk compensation first."

Of course.

Timothy listened to the options. The only way to get the information immediately was to give Tompkins his credit card number.

"Eight hundred dollars," Timothy said. "That's—very reasonable."

"You'd be alone in that opinion."

Tompkins told him that Leah was in Tennessee, employed at UT Knoxville, and living in a condo rental out on the edge of one of the many suburban neighborhoods surrounding the city. He gave Timothy the address and the name of the condo community. He also gave him the phone numbers of the Religion Department and Leah's office at the university.

"I assume you already have her cell number."

"I do, but she blocked me, I think. Either that or she's just ignoring my calls."

"In your life you're never going to need another skip tracer, but keep my card anyway," Tompkins said and hung up.

Man oh man. Tennessee. Tenn-a-freaking-see. I haven't worked here long enough to ask for time off. I'm going to have to straight-up quit this job.

And for what? To go down to Tennessee? And say what? I quit my crap job for you. I think I love you, if I even know what love is?

I miss your body in my bed.

Yeah, tell her that, dumbass. That'll do the trick.

Damn!

*****

After he'd stomped the hallways of Metropolitan in frustration and doubt, he went to Roger's office and quit. Effective immediately. He gave no notice. Roger shook his head. They were both grown men, both had Yale MBAs. Both knew what kind of a hole Timothy was digging for himself.

"Just tell me it's not about the woman, Tim," Roger said.

"It's the woman, Roger."

"God help you."

"I appreciate the sentiment. Interested in renting my house?"

Roger wasn't, so Timothy spent the next day packing for Tennessee and arranging for a house sitter.

He also decided to get rid of his car. *My beautiful Cadillac XTS.* In all his thinking, his remembering her departure, her walking out, he'd come to the conclusion that at least part of what she wanted to put behind her was his money. His money! Not that he could even remotely understand that. Timothy really didn't get people's opposition to wealth. Their envy? Their hatred of the rich and privileged? Sure, he got that. *But to oppose wealth on principle?* In any case, he wanted her to understand that he wasn't rich anymore. He'd left his father's firm. He didn't drive a Cadillac. He was unemployed!

I'm unemployed.

He didn't go to his Cadillac dealer. He went to a used car lot on the edge of town. When he pulled onto the lot, everyone who worked there came out of their offices and body shops and oil pits and walked around the car, wiping their greasy hands on rags and nodding appreciatively.

Their admiration of the car and the wealth behind the car gave him serious pause. But he persevered.

"I'm looking to trade," Timothy said to no one in particular.

There was a communal *huh?*

A dangerously overweight man who'd already sweated through his collar stepped up and said, "Trade for what?"

"I'm not sure." Timothy hesitated. "I want to impress a girl."

"And somehow this vehicle is not cutting the mustard?"

"Well—"

"Son, if she ain't impressed with this, I can tell you right now there ain't nothing on this lot that's gonna do the trick."

Uh huh, I know that's right, and *truth,* the men said and slowly returned to their work.

"I'm thinking maybe that pickup truck right there," and Timothy as he pointed to a faded red Chevy Silverado with a baby-blue front panel.

The man looked from Timothy to the pickup to the Cadillac and back to Timothy.

"Who is it you're trying to impress? Reba McEntire?"

"Who's that?"

"If you say so. Now what are you looking for? An even trade?"

"What's the truck going for?"

"Blue book's sixty-five," the man said without missing a beat.

"So, you're thinking straight up trade, eighty thousand-dollar Cadillac for a sixty-five-hundred-dollar rattle trap."

"It's a dog eat dog world."

Timothy said, "No. I mean, obviously no. Let's take this truck for a drive while you think about what else you're going to give me for the Caddy."

In the end, Timothy took the deed to the lot and the truck in exchange for the Cadillac. The deal was that when the man sold the Caddy, he would pay Timothy fifteen thousand and get the deed back. The man was getting the deal of a lifetime, he'd make thirty-five, maybe forty thousand when it all came down to it, but what could Timothy do? If he was going to be with Leah, he was going to have to change his ways.

Maybe not all of them. The dashboard was fuzzed with dust, and the cab smelled like fast-food hamburgers and ass. He left the truck at a detailing place and walked down to a Salvation Army store a couple of blocks away. He was carrying a suitcase. His worst one. The one he'd taken to camp when he was twelve. *Why did I save this?*

Well, now you know, don't you?

In terms of clothes, Timothy had brought only two pairs of jeans from his house. Not the designer ones, but the Levis and the Wranglers he'd bought for a camping weekend in the Taconic Mountains. He couldn't find a single shirt other than tee shirts he wanted to show up at Leah's place with. So, in the Salvation Army store he shopped for shirts. He'd already picked out four, faded and threadbare, when he looked at the prices. For what he'd paid for the shirt he was wearing, he could have bought sixty Salvation Army shirts. At the checkout, he pulled the white Canali dress shirt over his head and asked the cashier to throw it away or sell it, whatever seemed right. She stared at his pecs and abs with her mouth open. Then she leaned over the counter and looked him up and down and asked if he wanted to trade out his britches too while he was at it. He pulled on a blue work shirt that was as soft as flannel from a thousand washings and loaded his suitcase with the other shirts and pants he'd bought, and then he left.

When they brought the truck around, it looked no different. Even a coat of wax was useless. The foreman shrugged and said they had done the best they could. The interior was much, much improved, though. The seats and windows were clean, and the dashboard gleamed with a polished shine. He stopped at a convenience store and bought a cooler, a bag of ice, soft drinks and some plastic-wrapped sandwiches and chips.

I might as well get used to eating shit, literally and figuratively.

He took some enjoyment loading the cooler and heaving it over into the back of his truck. It felt kind of—virile? Manly? He went back into the store and bought a blue and white cap with a marlin on it. And a Black Ice Little Tree air-freshener to hang from the rearview mirror. Then he headed toward Interstate 95. It was pretty much a straight shot to Tennessee, interstate all the way. When he got as far as Knoxville, he'd let his phone tell him how to get to her apartment.

When a menagerie of rejection scenarios flashed though his mind, Timothy had to pull over and catch his breath.

I have crashed my whole world for her and what if it's not enough?

Deep breaths. Many deep breaths and then he thought, *I can always go back and run a used car lot. I am a part owner, after all.*

He laughed at the thought. He laughed at himself. He felt much better. Maybe if he didn't take himself so seriously, Leah would.

CHAPTER SIX

It would be frightening to think that in all the Cosmos,
which is so harmonious, so complete and equal to itself,
that only human life is happening randomly,
that only one's destiny lacks meaning.
~Mircea Eliade

Around four in the afternoon of the third day, Leah and Effie arrived at the front gate of the Greymont. Leah pulled out her phone and told Effie she had to look up the gate code.

Effie grabbed her side and groaned. It felt like a thorn, a big black thorn, was protruding through the seatback into her side. It was a *marking*, but not like any one she ever got before. She had known this was coming, had known ever since Leah called her. It was the main reason she'd agreed to come live with the girl. Over the phone, when Leah called, Effie had *marked* something, something coming through the phone line, almost a sound, in the background, a hissing, a miserable sound, a lamentation, like wind howling in a graveyard.

Leah carried Effie's suitcase and took her arm as they climbed the stairs to the apartment. When she unlocked the door and stepped inside, Leah gasped.

"Whew," Effie said. "It's a might humid in here."

"Did I leave the windows open? Whoa! Look at this philodendron!"

"Not likely, little girl."

"It's got to be twice the size it was when I left."

"That doesn't sound right."

"And this fuchsia. It's almost touching the floor. Did some kind of Miracle Gro Miracle come to pass here while I was gone?"

It wasn't the plants that caught Effie's attention. She felt her way toward the second bedroom, the small one.

"Plants aren't supposed to be thriving in the fall, are they? Aren't they supposed to be waning at this point in the Earth's tilt?"

"What's in here," she said.

"Well, that's your bedroom, if it suits you."

"Anywhere suits me, but this isn't just a bedroom, is it?"

"Well, yeah it is. I mean, it lets out onto the little balcony there."

"Yes. The balcony," and Effie felt her way to the sliding glass door and fumbled with the lock, finally clicking it loose and pulling the door open.

A rich, wet, fetid odor seeped in on the cool breeze. It wasn't that different from the rich, wet, fetid odor in the apartment, except that it was cooler. They stepped out onto the balcony.

Effie swept her arm across the horizon and said, "All woods out there, right?"

"Right."

Effie took Leah's hand and pressed it to her chest.

"Something's not right out there. You know that, don't you?"

"I'm beginning to."

They went back into the little bedroom and Leah showed Effie where everything was. Leah helped Effie put away her belongings and organize her bedside table. Effie tried all the pillows in the house until she found the two she wanted. One of them was Leah's favorite, but she didn't say anything. She just let Effie have it.

Effie and Leah cooked supper together. They fried some pork chops and made some beans and a salad. Effie declined a glass of wine and went to bed around eight.

Though she was worn out from the trip, she had trouble falling asleep. She could *mark* those woods in back of the place so clearly. There was nothing good about them. That she knew for sure.

What would be the danger to Leah and herself of just burning them down?

*****

Leah lay in bed staring at the ceiling and sucking her thumb. She had thought the prick she'd gotten was healing. The little scab was almost gone when she picked Effie up out in Oklahoma. But when she pulled up to the gates of the Greymont, her thumb started throbbing and she saw that it was swollen and red again.

She considered calling Timothy.

Why? Is there something you can't handle? Something Timothy can do that you can't? Are you Cinderella, Snow White? Little Red?

But really, she was thinking that it might be nice just to hear his voice. He could be a prig sometimes, but other times, mostly when they were alone, he was a great guy. Sometimes he acted and talked like he looked. Which is to say, beautiful. Good. Ideal, really. On the outside, he was everything she wanted. A Greek god.

Who gets to have all that in one man?

And sometimes, he was everything she wanted on the inside too. Everything she wanted from a human being.

Sometimes.

Maybe I can work with that.

Her friend Elizabeth said that you can never find a perfect man, that there are no perfect men, that men are essentially larger versions of little boys, stomping their feet and yelling for their mommies. They are nose-picking, ass-scratching, whiny, self-centered knots of id—until a woman takes one on as a project.

"You don't really think that Dudley was this fine figure of a man before I took him on, do you?" Elizabeth said.

"Dud's a great guy."

"Yeah, now. After four years of hard work. On my part. When I found him, he was laid up in a frat house, three sheets to the wind, spilling bong water on the shirt he hadn't changed in a week. Whatever he is now, I made him that."

"You're exaggerating."

"You think? Well, not by much. You think Timothy's got potential. It's your job to bring it out. Men rarely bring it out on their own."

She fell asleep with the image of Timothy emerging wet and naked from the shower in her mind. In her dreams, she did philosophy: in her dreams she thought about finding a man. The dream logic ran a familiar pattern: do I even need a man? Why would I need a man? What does it mean to have a man? Is every man going to try to be the boss of me? You could find a man to be the boss of. You could be the boss of Quentin. You might even be able to be the boss of Timothy. You could never be the boss of the arrowhead boy. And is that what you want? To be the boss? Is there no possibility of partnership? Can two people be equals in a relationship? Is that even possible, psychologically, financially, emotionally?

In the way of dreams, she found herself kissing a man. His lips were soft, his beard scratchy, his tongue probing. His body was hard, heavy, scratchy like bark. She opened her eyes and saw his. Green eyes. Gleaming emerald, green, greener than any eyes in the history of green eyes. Deep green, with golden flecks. With black flecks. With red flecks. Red flecks?

Then she woke up.

Her feet were cold. Cold air was passing over her feet like a fan was on them, and they were out from under the covers.

She tried to kick her covers down over her feet, but she couldn't move her legs.

Was she awake? She didn't feel awake or asleep. Maybe something in between. Maybe more asleep than awake because her stomach was churning with that nightmarish feeling where you're waiting for something bad that you just know is going to happen. She felt a panicky sensation in her chest. She decided to open her eyes, get herself oriented, wake completely up, shake off the now increasing feeling of panic, of terror.

If you're awake, then open your eyes. Just let them open.

It wasn't so easy. Her eyelids felt incredibly heavy. She could feel the weight of them on her face, like cold silver dollars.

She tried to relax.

You're in the slipstream of a bad dream. Just wake up!

What was that sound? So faint. What is that? A buzzing sound. Like—what? Some alarm clock she didn't own. And coming from under her bed!

Take a deep breath. Get it together, girl.

Finally, she was able to open her eyes.

Her bedroom was glowing.

Green. A strange, alien, outer spacey green. She wondered if maybe the streetlight was going bad, turning odd colors before it finally blew out altogether, but then remembered that there was no streetlight outside her window. Her window faced east, away from the parking lot, toward the woods, the dark woods. She could almost feel them, the trees, the bushes, the fallen leaves, out there, like a presence, like an emanation. The ceiling, awash in green light, was swirling like oil on water. But green. The room smelled like a bag of topsoil. She wanted to sit up but couldn't move.

You're dreaming. You've got to be dreaming.

Get up. Go wash your face. Wake up!

But she couldn't move. She couldn't even move one finger.

Her thumb throbbed. Painfully.

The buzzing sound modulated toward a more—scratchy sound. And got louder.

She couldn't move at all. Frozen. Paralyzed. Like she was dead. But her heart was beating. In fact, it was beating so hard that it hurt. Was it going to burst?

Could that happen? She thought, *This is what it's like to be dead, to be at the gates of Hell.*

Am I dying?

It seemed like all the air had been sucked out of the room. She couldn't get a deep breath, but she was panting, hyperventilating.

The room was getting darker.

Is that someone standing in the door?

She wanted to scream. She tried to shout, but nothing came out of her mouth.

A shadow crossed the ceiling. Something was in the room!

She squeezed her eyes shut.

She could hear someone breathing. Something breathing.

The bed shifted. It felt like it was going to turn over. As if some huge someone had sat down on it.

No. Someone definitely sat down on it!

The sound in the room was a hissing now. Whoever was sitting on the bed was hissing. Like a snake.

Open your eyes!

No no no no no.

Then a hand fell on her chest. A big hand, pressing down. Hard. Pushing the air out of her lungs.

She couldn't catch her breath. The hand was sinking into her chest like dough. She could feel the nails—the claws — tearing through her lungs! The fingers closed around her heart and squeezed. The world shrunk to a fist-sized pain in her chest. She felt emptied, like a deer hung up and gutted. She felt cold inside, like cold air blowing on her exposed organs. She tried her best to scream.

Open your eyes!

The light came on in the room and Effie was standing just inside the door.

"Sweetie? Are you okay? I think you might be having a bad dream. I can hear you crying over in my room."

Leah was soaked in sweat.

"Yes. Yes, I had a bad dream. God! It was so real."

She looked around the room. Nothing was out of place.

Except.

"Here, Effie. Let me help you back to bed."

"I'm okay. I can find my way around here pretty good now."

Leah took her back to her room and got her settled. She checked the latch on the door to the balcony. It was locked, of course.

Back in her own room, Leah looked at the top of her bookcase. Here she had arranged some of her relics, things she'd brought back from her travels to the evil places she hoped to write her book about: a stem of mug wort from the Sea of Trees in Japan, a small piece of bone from Kabayan, a blue stone from Teotihuacan, all smuggled in her luggage. She was lucky not to be in a foreign prison somewhere. She had arranged these items into a little—what? —shrine? No. That's not the right word. *Or is it?* It's not like she worshipped these things.

They were evil.

And then she realized it. She had brought evil into her own home. And now something else was going on too. Something coming out of those woods behind her apartment. Something that came into her very room.

And put its hand on her!

*****

The next day, while Leah napped, Effie made her way carefully down the steps of the apartment building. They were made of concrete and steel, so it wouldn't do to fall. She didn't like the cane but had brought it since she really didn't know where she was going. Except that she was going around back, to *mark* those woods behind the apartment.

Somebody had planted some gardenia bushes nearby. The smell was cloying.

Why is it blooming now, so late in the year?

And maybe, was that summer sweet clethra nearby? That was nicer.

She stepped off the sidewalk into the grass and headed toward the back of the building.

As soon as she turned the corner, she *marked* those woods. *Lord have mercy. The* marking *was so strong it almost knocked her down. It was almost like the woods were* marking *her.* It was like the screech of a thousand burning hawks falling out of the sky, and the smell of poisoned rats. Tin foil on your fillings, pepper sauce in your eye. She almost turned back, but she could sense the wall just ahead. Leah had told her about the wall, about the little girl.

When Effie got within about a foot of the wall, she touched it with her cane. The wall seemed to hiss at her. But the cicadas were rioting around her, and she couldn't be sure if what she was hearing was real.

She *marked* a door in the wall, right in front of her. Why hadn't Leah mentioned the door.

Well, she might not have seen it, Effie thought.

She knocked her cane against it. It was covered with vines and whatnot. She was hesitant to reach out her hand and feel for a knob to the door. Something was seriously amiss out here.

*****

Leah woke from her nap with a nagging headache. The air seemed charged somehow and there was a hissing sound, like cicadas or tinnitus or something. When she tried to stand up, she felt dizzy and sat back down on the bed.

After a few deep breaths, she rose carefully and crept to the kitchen, steadying herself on the wall as she went. She stood at the refrigerator drinking cold water with the door open.

She felt better.

"Effie," she called.

Nothing.

She stuck her head in Effie's room. The bed was made, empty. Effie was not in the apartment.

Leah ran for the door, then turned back and opened the door to the balcony. Effie was down by the wall, about where the little girl had been. And like the little girl, Effie seemed frozen there, staring at the wall.

Staring? Are you an idiot? She's blind!

The wind was blowing cold air and scattering raindrops, bending the trees which waved like dancers. Just as she opened her mouth to call Effie, the wind picked up dramatically. It was shrieking now. Leaves and small limbs were flying and striking Leah as she leaned on the railing.

"Effie! Effie!" she called, but it was no use.

Is a tornado coming? Another one?

A limb broke off from the tree next to the building and hit the roof and slid down, falling onto the balcony. She stepped out of the way at the last second and slipped on the wet floor, going down hard on her butt.

Get inside before you get killed!

Effie!

She crawled to the railing and looked between the bars. Effie was staggering across the yard, buffeted by the wind. She must have lost her bearings for she was heading in the wrong direction. She called again, but it was pointless.

Effie stepped wrong or something and fell. It began raining in earnest. Effie would be soaked. Leah had to get her. The floor of the balcony was slippery as ice. Leah was having trouble getting to her feet. Effie too was trying to get up, but she kept slipping.

Then Leah saw the tree.

On the other side of the wall a half-dead tree was leaning precariously over the wall, pushed by the wind. It looked like it was going to fall. And Effie was right under it!

Leah went for the sliding door and slipped again on the wet floor. She crawled into the apartment, then got to her feet and ran out of the apartment. She took the steps two at a time and headed around to the back of the building.

Effie was still on her hands and knees, and the tree was creaking over, leaning at an untenable angle.

Leah sprinted toward her but caught her foot on something—or did something catch her?—and she slid up beside Effie, headfirst, like a runner stealing second base.

"C'mon," Leah said and pulled Effie to her feet.

They walked soaking wet through the drenched grass and stood next to the back of the building, trying to catch their breath. The wind blew so hard they could barely keep their feet, and the tree gave one mighty groan and crashed through the wall and onto the ground where Effie had just been.

"What was that?" Effie said.

"Tree fell. Knocked down part of the wall."

"Where the door was?"

"What door?"

"Never mind. Let's get inside and out of this, for mercy's sake."

Back in the apartment, Leah said she needed a hot shower and asked Effie if she wanted to go first.

Effie declined.

"I'm getting into some warm pajamas," she said.

Leah turned on the water as hot as she could stand it and stood in the steamy spray, trying to shake off the deep cold. She washed her hair, and while she worked in the conditioner, she thought about Timothy. She stood there letting the conditioner work, the scent of lilac filling the steamy bath, she ran her hands, still coated in conditioner, over her breasts. Her nipples stood up, and she squeezed them. Timothy loved her breasts. His foreplay focused on them. He did go down on her, and he was pretty good down there, but there was no doubt in her mind that he was marking time with his tongue until he could climb up her body and get at the titties, as he called them.

Bottle baby, she thought, and slipped her hand down between her legs. *You can condition pubes as well as hair.*

She hadn't really found her rhythm when she heard Effie banging around in the kitchen. She sighed, washed out her hair, climbed out, and toweled dry.

*****

Timothy sat in his pickup truck in the parking lot of the Salvation Army. He'd come to the fork in the road. The old joke said he should take it. His stomach was churning, and he was dizzy with indecision. The trip to Knoxville was twelve hours, or so Google said. That estimate was probably based on a best-case scenario: no traffic, no bad weather, no stopping for food or the restroom. No need for sleep. A long ass ride.

What he needed was to talk to her. To hear her voice. He needed some encouragement. He picked up his cell phone.

She's not going to answer if she sees your number.

He looked around the parking lot. Maybe he could borrow someone's phone.

And what would you say if someone randomly asked to use your phone at the Salvation Army?

On the other hand, nothing ventured. He stepped out of the Silverado and looked around. In the back corner of the parking lot, under some overhanging trees, was a pay phone.

A pay phone!

And the damn thing was like brand new. It accepted his credit card.

Timothy punched in her number, reading it off his smart phone.

She's probably not going to answer a number she doesn't recognize any more than she's going to answer my number.

"Hello?"

"It's me," he said.

"Timothy," she said.

To hear her say his name!

Man, I need to see her, he thought. *Damn, just her voice. I would give anything I own if I could look into her eyes right now.*

"What number are you calling me from?"

"I lost my phone in the truck somewhere," he said.

"In the what? Did you say 'truck'? What truck?"

"My Chevy Silverado"

"Your Chevy silver-what?"

"Silverado. Look, I know you've been avoiding me. But—"

"Something's going on, Timothy. Something strange. I don't know how to explain it."

"What? You sound scared. Are you scared of something?"

"I don't know. Something is going on with the plants."

"The plants? What, what plants?"

"I know, I know. It sounds crazy. I may be going crazy. I may be going out of my flipping mind. And taking my grandmother with me."

"You've got Effie with you?"

"You remembered her name. That's so—I miss you, Timothy."

"Right back at you, sweetheart."

"Maybe you don't want me anymore. I wouldn't. I've screwed up so many things. You wouldn't believe how I lost my job at Yale."

"I might. I don't care anyway. Yale, Tennessee, whatever."

"I might end up teaching high school or something."

"Really. Not even community college. All the way down to high school. You must have messed up really good, Leah Grove."

"I think the woods behind my apartment may be trying to kill me. And I know how that sounds. Things have gotten so weird. Like I say, I'm losing it."

"Maybe not. You need to see this weird ass manuscript I found on Amazon. I think your father may be in it."

"My father's in it?"

"I think."

"What does it say?"

"Honestly, I couldn't tell you for sure. It's crazy. It's all about the intelligence of plants, the moral superiority of the vegetable world, crazy stuff like that. Oh, and it talks about some Dr. Grove, that could be your father, maybe, trying to combine ergot and some hallucinogenic plant from South America so that he could eat it and talk to the ergot. Like the ergot was a god or something."

"Wow. Do you have that book?"

"If you can call it that."

"Where are you?"

"At a pay phone outside a convenience store just south of Roanoke, Virginia."

"What's a pay phone?"

"Look, I'm on my way to you."

"You don't even know where I am."

"Um, yeah, I do. Don't get mad now, but I had somebody track you down."

"I'm not mad. I'm glad. I almost called you last night. I wish I had, to tell you the truth. But—"

"What?"

"I don't know if you want to get involved in this."

"And what? Leave you and your grandmother to deal with—whatever the hell is going on?"

"When you put it like that—"

Then he said, "I've missed you so much."

"You've missed me in your bed."

"Okay. I'm not even going to try to deny that. But I've missed you. *You*, Leah. Have you missed me?"

"In bed, maybe."

They laughed.

"Look. You need to know. I don't have any money. I quit my job. I told my father to let Eddie handle everything."

"You quit your job?"

"Yeah. Then I got another one."

"Oh. That's good. I guess."

"Then I quit that one."

"Just in a quitting mood?"

"I can get a job in Tennessee. I can get a job anywhere. Doing anything. I still have the equity in my house. I can sell that."

"Maybe you are still rich."

"And if worse comes to worse, I can pawn this bent spoon I've been carrying around with me like a lucky charm."

"Oh. I uh—"

"You can explain that some other time. I'm getting on the road right now. I'll see you in twelve or thirteen hours. Try to wait on me."

"I'll be looking for you."

*****

The next day when Leah got up Effie had breakfast ready.

"What time did you get up?"

"Crack of dawn, I suppose," Effie said. "Old folks tend to be early risers."

"How do you manage to fry such perfect eggs? I don't do this well and I can see."

"Frying is mostly a hearing thing."

"Right, of course. Look, you got any idea what's going on here?"

"Something's not right in those woods out there, if that's what you mean."

"Yeah, that's what I mean. That tree tried to fall on you. Deliberately."

"I wouldn't go that far. But something out there doesn't like you very much."

"Me? You mean 'me' personally?"

Effie said, "Yes, you. Leah Grove. Has it escaped your attention that your name, Grove, means 'woods'? This is a situation of same calling to same."

"'Same calling to same'. You're saying that something out there is the same as me?"

"In some way, yes."

"And my name cannot have anything to do with it. My name is purely chance."

"As a graduate of the Yale college, do you even believe in pure chance? Is that even allowed in the Yale college?"

"Stop saying 'the Yale college'. And, yes, even Yale might have room for chance."

"In what department, I'm wondering. Not religion. Not science. Y'all got a department of blackjack?"

"Fine. You win. Let's talk about these woods."

"Maybe you should tell me about them. Aren't you the one who traipsed all over the world on Yale's dime studying evil places?"

Indeed, Leah had. She had stood in the Aokigahara Forest, listening to the bamboo moan, by the blood-soaked Pyramid of the Sun at Teotihuacan where the wind whispered in her ears. And she'd felt something. Something vague, something nebulous, something that she sensed to be evil.

But nothing like this.

The house plants were now trailing on the floor, blooming in the chilling weather of autumn. Some horrible thing had come out of those woods and into her room and sat on her chest while she slept. And, whatever Effie said, Leah knew damn well that tree had waited until Effie was helpless on the ground before it fell right where she would have been if Leah hadn't gotten there in time.

Effie said, "Maybe you should wait on your man to get here."

"My man? What man?"

"You'd be the one to know his name."

"What makes you think I have a man? Do I look like I have a man? Is there a man somewhere around here?"

"Not that I've seen."

"Funny."

"So—you're saying you don't have a man."

"What do you think?" Leah said.

"I think you have a man, a man you're missing a lot. A man you think about a lot. And I think he's on his way here now."

"How do you know that?"

"I *marked* it."

"You—"

And then Effie told her the story of her *marking*.

It all sounded so familiar to Leah, or—it felt familiar to her. While what Leah felt in certain places—good and evil—wasn't exactly what Effie was describing as her marking, there was something, something similar, like same calling to same.

"And here's something else I've *marked*. All this traveling around you've done, you've drawn notice. You've gotten on something's radar, and things are coming to a head. Right here. Right now. There are other places where this conjunction could have happened, a deserted city, a dark lake. But this is the nearest, now and in these woods. And here is where it will happen."

"Where what will happen?"

"That I don't know, child. But something. Something."

"I have to go somewhere today."

"I figured. And you don't want to wait on your man?"

"Timothy."

"The saint of that name gave up everything to follow Paul. Forsook his family, his life, his home for the love of Paul. And of Christ Jesus."

"My Timothy is not religious, so much."

"Yet his sacrifice is considerable."

"What sacrifice?"

"I'm not sure. You can ask him when he gets here."

And after that, you're going to have to take him to a motel, Leah thought. *What you're going to do to him is gonna be all kinds of loud, and* that *Effie flat out doesn't need to hear!*

*****

The Road of Remembrance had grown up since her first visit. Leah could barely distinguish where the tire ruts had been. She tripped a couple of times over vines that had grown across the road. What was certain was that no vehicle had been down this way in a long time. Mr. Patchett had an old car parked next to his trailer when she came the first time, though it had been pretty well covered with fallen leaves, suggesting he hadn't driven it in a while. Clearly, he was not driving it at all now.

When she came in sight of the trailer park, she drew herself up a bit. The two trailers other than Patchett's that had been occupied were clearly no longer so. One was gone and the other was tilted at an unlivable angle. She could see a huge root underneath, pushing up on one side and threatening to tip it over altogether.

Patchett's car was still next to the trailer. She called out to him, then stepped onto the little porch and knocked on the door. Dead quiet. No wind disturbed the leaves, no bird song, no squirrels chittering in the limbs of the trees. She knocked again. No answer.

Leah sat in one of the lawn chairs she'd sat in on her first visit. She thought she could use that cold Coke he'd promised her on her return. It was a gray day. The air was thick with mist under the trees, a hint of wood smoke in it. The trunks of the trees were gray against gray. What she could see of the sky between the limbs was gray. The day felt heavy with rain.

On the little table where she'd set her Coke last time was a notebook. Spiral bound. Faded red cover. She picked it up carefully. It was swollen with damp, the pages wrinkly and bent. Smeary ballpoint handwriting covered every page. There were some drawings and lots of numbered lists. It had no discernible order.

She guessed it was the history of this little trailer park Mr. Patchett said he was writing. The first pages detailed Patchett's moving here. There were descriptions of the woods, dimensions of the park, of his trailer, a convoluted description of the orientation of his trailer to the other trailers in the park. Finally, a map that clarified all of that. He had gotten, somehow, a place near the front of the park, close to the road.

Leah was surprised at how big the place had been back then when Patchett had first moved in. When she'd been here before, it seemed that even at its peak occupancy, the park was no more than ten trailers, but this map showed upward of forty sites.

She flipped forward into the middle of the book and found another map. This one showed the shrinking he'd talked about. If the book could be trusted, Patchett had been right. The woods indeed seemed to be pushing the trailer park and its inhabitants out of existence, for it was the sites deepest in the woods, farthest from the road, that disappeared first. Another map toward the end of the book showed just five sites left, including Patchett's own, the ones closest to the road.

A chill ran down her spine, and she felt as if she were being watched. It was probably just the cold damp mist that now was visibly falling between the gray trunks of the trees and shining on the leaves of the underbrush just across the little unused road. She knew what Effie would say.

*Y*ou're definitely being watched.

Where was Patchett? Maybe gone to the grocery? His car hadn't been moved in months, that was obvious. So, he must walk to the grocery. She leaned back in the chair and opened the notebook toward the end.

Today, Old Man Hollingsworth has loaded up his truck. He came over after locking down the trailer and shook my hand. Going to live with his daughter and her husband down in Alabama somewhere he said. Enough of this goddamn place, was what he told me. Tired of fixing that broke down trailer ever damn day. The oak tree what fell on his back porch was apparently the last straw. After he left, I went over and looked at that porch. It was busted to smithereens, and the old man hadn't bothered to drag it off and cut it up. Can't say I blame him. Another casualty of these strange woods.

She looked around and shivered again. There wasn't a soul around. She got up and walked around Patchett's trailer. Nothing had changed since her last visit, except the underbrush had taken over his little backyard and was now all the way up to and against the back of his trailer. She peered through the bushes. It looked as if some of the limbs had somehow pushed through the back wall of Patchett's trailer.

Was that even possible?

She turned and looked west through the woods and was tempted to light out toward where she knew the back wall of the complex had to be, just as she'd planned to do on her first trip. She took a couple steps in that direction when she realized she was still holding Mr. Patchett's notebook.

She knew what he'd say if he was here.

Don't go.

And she certainly wasn't going to have him come home and find she'd taken his history with her. She didn't even want him to know she'd opened it without his permission, so she picked her way back around to the front and stepped onto the porch again.

That was when she noticed his front door wasn't completely shut. The particle board the door was made of had swollen and busted open, making it impossible to shut completely.

"Mr. Patchett?"

Leah sat down and opened the book again.

There were some drawings of leaves and stems and flowering parts, stamens and whatnot, stuff she couldn't name.

Who takes Botany in college?

Then he started writing again.

When a man's born, when he takes a wife, and as he is borne to his final resting place, you'll find that his fellows have surrounded him with flora. A man will use flowers in his courting, and he'll decorate his supping table with them. Who imagines Heaven without flowers? Who could imagine Earth without them? Plants probably don't need us, but we sure need them. Our clothes and food and homes come from the plant world. You'll not hear a note from violin without what some tree made it possible. This paper I write on, the pages of Moby Dick, *the paper I wrote a poem to Cheryl Nations on in the tenth grade on, this is all plants.*

She pried apart the pages closest to the end of the book. Some stuck together and tore when she tried to separate them. She felt bad about it.

Why did he leave it out here in the damp?

And I alone am left to tell the tale. After Hollingsworth left, it was only me and Miss Tammy Letty left. And now she's gone, packed up and gone to a nursing home on the west side of Knoxville. Put there by her kids. Probably for the best. Nobody here to look out for her the way she needs looking after. And while it's a fact that I moved out here in the first place to get some breathing room, some peace from the crush of people in the Army and in town, now there's no one left. But I am still not alone. There is something here, something ancient, something malign. I figured that when I died, the book would never close. That someone would find it and continue it, but these woods are writing the ending for me. They're coming back.

That seemed to be the end of it. Maybe he moved away. Like everybody else out here had.

But why did he leave the book behind?

Behind her the door, the warped and broken door, creaked as the wind pushed it farther open. She rose from the old lawn chair and stepped up to the door and pushed it wide open. The air was musty. It smelled like dirt, like rotting leaves. When she stepped into the trailer, the floor felt soft under her feet, like she might fall through at any moment. Super dark, spots of light here and there. The soft floor was freaking her out.

She felt her way to the window and pulled the curtains open. They were rotted and came apart in her hands and she dropped them on the floor and shook her hands. *Yuck.* A couch, a chair. A bookcase with wet and swollen paperbacks, sprouting leafy tendrils. Three framed pictures hanging on the wall: a couple, probably his parents, a little boy with a bicycle. Maybe him? A group of soldiers standing around a truck. Vietnam, no doubt.

How long has he been gone? Did he think to take nothing with him?

She wanted to check the bedroom, to see if he'd at least taken his clothes with him. The narrow hallway pressed in around her, heavy with a stale, musty air that clung to her skin. She opened one door—bathroom. Empty. Then the other—

Bedroom.

There were no curtains on the window, just harsh light pouring in, illuminating the horror before her.

Mr. Patchett was there. Against the wall. No—*on* the wall.

His limbs jutted grotesquely through his chest, splayed as if pinned in place. Thick vines coiled around his body, anchoring him like some obscene trophy. A gnarled branch thrust from his mouth, bark hardened along his veins. And from the hollowed sockets of his eyes, delicate flowers bloomed.

She staggered back out of the room, down the hall, out the door, running, gasping, falling, up, holding on to a tree trunk. She closed her eyes, but all she could see was Patchett, torn open, bound by vines to the wall, half man, half plant.

She shuddered.

How could this even happen?

It's not like he was sitting in a chair, dead, and then got covered up by moss and lichen. Something reached into his home and ripped him apart. Something tore through the wall and killed him.

She reached for her phone to call 911, but her pocket was empty. She looked around on the ground where she fell, then traced her steps back to the trailer.

Maybe it's in the hall or in there with Patchett.

Curlicues of ivy wound into his hair.

Forget it then. You're not even going back in there.

She would call from home. It was a long way down the Road of Remembrance to the main drag and back to the apartment. Surely it would be closer if she struck out through the woods and did what she came here to do in the first place: see the wall from this side. Maybe from this side she could see the door that Effie *marked.*

Look, you fool. Look at what these woods did to Patchett. He warned you. He should have taken his own warning. Do you want to end up like him?

She dragged one of the lawn chairs off Patchett's little porch and sat across the grassy road from his trailer.

This would be easier if Timothy were here.

And that thought pissed her off.

Get over yourself, Cinderella. There's a blind woman at your house who's not afraid of anything.

In truth, she wanted to head out into the woods. She wanted to the first time she came, and she wanted to now.

Why?

She felt alone and yet watched. The woods were alive. Of course, they were alive. But there was something else. Something about the draw of this place, the invitational nature of danger, of defeat, and ultimately of death. It was a part of her, to seek out menace and risk and peril.

What you want is to meet the darkness as fully as the light.

*****

A twelve-hour drive. Well, maybe. Timothy wondered if he could drive straight through. He was getting a late start, so most of the long drive would be in the dark. Of course, it was interstate driving, so no redlights, no stop signs, no little speed trap towns. Of course, it also meant that it was going to be monotonous. Sleep-inducing. He could just drive until he was tired, grab a motel room, and drive the rest of the way tomorrow. What's the big hurry?

Her, you idiot.

She said she needed you.

And that's because the woods behind her house are out to get her?

Timothy pulled out of the parking lot and headed toward I-95. He wished he had some book on tape or something. The Silverado had a CD player. He should have looked around in the Salvation Army for some CDs.

Too late now. Maybe instead you can spend the time thinking about how you are going to deal with, for that matter, make a life with a crazy person. A person who believes that the plant world is coming after her. That the plant world is involved with good and evil.

For that matter, you can try to figure out if she even wants to make a life with you.

On the phone she had been saying exactly what the crazy man who wrote the "book" he'd paid sixty-six dollars for said. That the plant world was conscious, was thinking, was acting with will, and capable of evil.

Good God.

Maybe Leah will write a book that she staples together with notebook paper, and she'll sell it on Amazon, or maybe at a garage sale.

Timothy shook his head. It would be easy to turn the truck around and head back to his house. To straighten the bent spoon and slide it into the back of a drawer somewhere, to forget about it. Forget about Leah.

No, that would not be easy.

The truck wasn't much to look at, but it rode smoothly, and he liked sitting higher than the drivers of the cars around him.

Maybe I can be this guy, the truck guy. If that's what she wants.

But that was the problem. Timothy straight up didn't know what she wanted. It was true that she had mocked his wealth at every turn. She enjoyed all the good food he bought her, his nice car, his beautiful house, but even her enjoyment of those things was tinged with sarcasm.

So, was it the money that ruined everything? Is that why she left?

Just admit it. You don't know why she left.

On the other hand, Leah definitely seemed glad to hear from him. She really seemed to want him to come to Knoxville; therefore, it couldn't have been about the money. She wanted him to come before he called her, before he told her about leaving everything behind in New Haven. Maybe it wasn't the money at all.

Timothy hated to admit it, but maybe that jackass Maxwell was right. Maybe the real problem was that he didn't have a clue who Leah Grove truly was. She was a woman who believed in Good and Evil—who *saw* the world in a way Timothy didn't. *Couldn't.* She sensed something beyond the physical, refused to believe that what they could touch and see was all there was.

What was it Maxwell said? Numinous?

At a red light a block from the entrance to I-95, he Googled numinous.

"Filled with or characterized by a sense of a supernatural presence. 'a numinous place.'"

So, Timothy didn't believe in the numinous. Was that the problem? Leah just couldn't be with someone so committed to the purely physical. Someone so shortsighted. Or maybe she pitied him. Pathetic money boy, trapped in the material world. Materialistic through and through. Maybe she couldn't love somebody that shallow.

Then again, she had never said she loved him. Not once. And to his everlasting grief, he'd never told her either. Whatever either of them felt, that word had never passed between them.

I'll rectify that soon enough.

And maybe he would. Except he wasn't sure exactly what love was. He had never been in love with a woman, this he knew. He had liked a lot of women, had been attracted to them. Had slept with them. But loved them? No.

So who had he ever loved? Not his father. He had wanted his father's approval. And maybe if he'd ever gotten it, he would have loved the man.

Is that how love works? Quid pro quo?

He had liked his older brother, Andrew. He was a great kid. Funny. Smart. Andrew had always looked out for Timothy.

Did I love him? I honestly don't know.

He certainly didn't love his brother, Eddie.

On the other hand, he had loved his mother. But is that helpful? He certainly didn't love his mother the way he loved

Leah. Are those emotions even the same thing? They have the same name, but they're really nothing alike.

Just admit it, dumbass. You have no idea what love is.

Was he so materialistic that he really thought love was a chemical reaction somewhere in the brain, in the limbic system, that his psychological makeup pretended was something else?

Do you love her or not, jackass?

And the answer was, of course, yes. Obviously, he loved her. But the only evidence he had of that was that he'd reached a point where he couldn't imagine life without her.

But isn't that really just about you? Your life, your feelings? Is love a hole that you fell into? You fell in love? Is that what being in love is? How do you make it about her? Love as you've practiced it is selfish. Your feelings.

That's what wife beaters say, isn't it? Yeah, I beat the living hell out of her, but I love her. I feel that love.

Oh my god.

The problem is this. Is love a noun or a verb?

If love is real, if it exists outside the material world, if it's something qualitatively different from chemistry and psychology, then why not evil plants? If love is possible, then anything is possible.

Watch the road, shit for brains. Don't get killed before you get there to help her fight evil.

Evil plants!

*****

Leah wanted Mr. Patchett's history of the trailer park. She had left it on the coffee table in the front room of his trailer. She carried the chair back to his porch, took a deep breath and pushed on the door.

But it didn't open.

What the—?

It wasn't closed flush. It was too swollen; but three vines had snaked down from the roof and wrapped around the door handle, pulling it tight.

Leah looked up. The vines had broken through the roof.

What? In the last fifteen minutes?

Adrenaline flashed through her like a lightning bolt. She threw her shoulder against the door over and over until it flew open, and she fell headlong into the room. She grabbed the notebook and ran out and around behind the trailer.

Damn! You should have at least looked for your phone.

What had Mr. Patchett said? Something about walking in a straight line, how hard that would be, holding a line, how easily she could become lost.

You should have brought a compass!

You don't have a compass.

The trailer next door was tipped over. It had belonged to Mr. Patchett's beautiful lady. *Gone the way of all things.* Leah climbed onto it and tried to see out into the woods, maybe the wall or the roofs of the Greymont. But she couldn't.

How far to the wall?

Well, it was probably a two mile walk on the roads from her apartment to Mr. Patchett's, so—what? A mile, mile and a half through the woods to the wall? Maybe? By tomorrow, Timothy would probably be here. She could hike it with him.

Pull it together, Snow White. You're a full-blooded woman. You do not need a man to protect you.

But maybe you need somebody.

It was cloudy, but she could see the faint gray sun and so had a pretty good idea which way west was. She started out through the trees. Pretty soon she was out from under the trees and clawing her way through some thick brush.

Patchett was right. She kept having to turn north or south to get around particularly knotty clumps of brush, and she tried to correct her path once she was around. It was getting cloudier, thick grumbly thunderheads muscling out the thin high clouds.

Was more rain coming? More trees falling?

But she could still see the sun. At least for a while.

Before her was a swampy bog and no way around it. She was soon up to her knees in scummy green water. Huge bullfrogs splashed away from her, and snakes swam around her legs. A root seemed to grab at her foot, and she fell into the water and almost lost Patchett's book. Now soaked, she shivered with cold and looked up at the sky. She could no longer tell where the sun was. Patchett had been right. She was lost.

Lost as a goose, Effie would say.

The ground slowly rose, and she traipsed through tightly grouped trees, sometimes barely able to scrape between them. Branches slapped at her face, and she finally could go no farther and had to back out and head in another direction.

How long till dark, she thought. *Are you going to end up walking all night? Can you find your way in the dark?*

No.

She closed her eyes as she pushed through some leafy bushes and slipped and fell down a small hill. When she got up, she thought she might be in a dream.

She was surrounded by brilliant, almost hallucinatory purple. Flowers that had no business blooming in the fall as far as she could see in every direction. As she began to push her way through the flowers, terrible thorns tore at her clothes and gouged jagged cuts in her hands and arms: bougainvillea.

My god, she thought. *This is not possible. This is some kind of nightmare.*

Every step she took was torture. She sacrificed her hands to keep the thorns from ripping out her eyes. Blood dripped down her arms. Thorns tore holes in her jeans, and her blood soaked the denim. A hawk screamed, then another, and then the air was filled with hawks, dozens of them, screeching, dive bombing her, brushing her head, clawing at her. She dropped to all fours and crawled, the ground carpeted in fallen thorns, thorns in her hands, her knees, her feet. Something hit her on the back. She turned and saw a rabbit, torn, gutted. It had dropped out of the sky. Then another hawk flew close and dropped a dead cat right in front of her. Disemboweled.

Thunder rumbled. Raindrops the size of severed thumbs fell on her face. Then lightning flashed. The rain beat down on her like fists. Before her were more thorns. Behind her thorns. She lay down on the thorny, soaking ground.

You're done, she thought. *Just give it up. The old man was right. You should not have come here.*

She rolled over and faced the sky. Blood and dirt rivered off her face. Thunder crashed so loudly she jumped and turning she saw a pine tree, struck by lightning and burning. Fiery limbs and branches fell and set the bushes below on fire.

Despite the rain, the fire grew and rushed toward her, consuming the bougainvillea like tissue paper.

Leah got to her feet and pushed her way through the great webs of thorns. Smoke burned her eyes, and she could feel hot ash burning the backs of her legs. She finally cleared the bougainvillea and found herself in piney woods, the ground covered with reddish gold straw. She turned and saw the fire racing toward her, burning tree and straw like they were soaked in gasoline. She ran as fast as she could, dodging through the trees. She jumped a small creek, tripped, and when she got up, could see the roofs of the Greymont in the distance. The wall had to be right ahead. Then she saw the dead tree. The one she could see from her balcony. The one that stood taller than the rest.

But something was going on.

Green twigs, leaves, tendrils were emerging from the gray bark, as if it were coming alive again. Except she could actually *see them growing!* Like time-lapse photography, the leaves were unfolding right before her eyes, new limbs emerging from the trunk, the whole thing going from gray to green.

She couldn't move. She was rooted to the spot before the tree.

A face was emerging from the bark. First the nose, then the chin, the eyes. The eyes burned red out of the green. On the mouth, the lips, a knowing smile. An evil smile.

Leah Grove.

The thing said.

Said. No. Not said. There was no sound. She suffered the words, deep in her chest, like a pain. Very like a pain.

The fire is coming, Leah Grove. Where will you go?

The words tightened her chest. She struggled to breathe. The tree morphed before her eyes. She fell to her knees. She opened her mouth wide, trying to breathe, trying to call out, trying to scream. A vine wrapped itself around her ankle.

The man emerging from the tree looked like the Green Man. Leah had seen the face of the Green Man on churches and public houses all over England and Ireland. He was the god of spring, the god of vegetation. He was renewal and birth.

But only for plants.

The fire is coming, Leah. It will burn you to ash. Ash and bone will be all that is left of you. But every tree and every bush will come back. We live in concert with fire. It cleanses us. We rise from it. But it is death for you. And when every man is burned off this planet, we will remain.

Is this what my father saw? When he ingested the ergot? When he ate the flesh and blood of the god he thought he had brought forth? Has the thing that took him and my mother now come for me?

You are an accident, Leah Grove. An anomaly. The animal is a perversion of the plant. And you, the thinking animal, the greatest perversion of all, you and all your kind are temporary. You will destroy yourselves, but you cannot destroy us. Even the beasts of the field serve us, spread out seed. Fire serves us, water serves us. We change one molecule and every mushroom poisons you, every fruit is toxic, every leaf deadly. Where are you then?

Where do you think bees got their hive minds? They move fast enough for you to see their workings. A plant may take 1000 years to make a decision, another ten thousand to implement it. A million to celebrate. We laugh. We hear our laughter bouncing back to us off the farthest galaxy.

You've filled the world with poison and radiation. Harmless to us, deadly to you. You've done us a favor. We grow without hindrance at Chernobyl. Do not try to eat the plants there, Leah Grove.

Rain can warp, swell, discolor, rust, loosen, mildew, stink, peel paint, consume wood, erode masonry, corrode metal, expand destructively when it freezes or seep into every crack when it evaporates. Everything that pulls you down and lifts us up.

Our seeds can fly, spin, bury themselves, float across oceans, sleep for a thousand years, spin through outer space.

Let a comet hit this world and you will all die, but our seed will scatter to the galaxies. We will never die. You are ephemeral, Leah Grove. We are eternal.

There is the western gate, Leah Grove. You, you thinking things, always headed west, into the sunset, Leah, the ever expanding West, out there, just beyond your reach, burning in the last fires of the sun, dying with the sun, out there, Leah. Go, for the winds are tearing you away. Go with yours.

The agony in her chest subsided.

The Green Man was gone and only the dead tree remained. A fiery limb fell next to her and burned her hand. The pain boosted her onto her feet, and she ran toward what she hoped was the wall. The fire was right on her heels.

"Leah! Leah!"

Effie was calling her. She headed toward her voice and found the wall.

"Effie! I'm here!"

"Get over here. The woods are on fire."

"No duh! I can't get over it."

"Use the door."

"What door? There's no door."

"There is too a door. I'm standing right in front of it."

Leah clawed at the vines, yanked them down, pulled them off the wall, and found the door. The handle was rusted, but she leaned on it with all her might. It gave way and the door popped open and she fell onto the Greymont lawn at Effie's feet.

The woods were consumed in flames, and the wind was blowing hot ash and burning limbs over the wall and into the yard. Huge flaming wreaths of pine needles flew over their heads and landed on the roof of the apartment building.

Leah pulled Effie's arm, and they hurried away from the wall.

"I think the apartment may burn down," Leah yelled.

"Let's not go in then," Effie said, reasonably.

They ran past the building and into the parking lot. They slowed to a quick walk, Leah holding tight to Effie.

Leah looked back at the woods. Burning limbs and pine straw lay on the roof of her building, but she realized that the roof was terra cotta and would not burn. They passed the first building in the complex and headed toward the front gate. There were four cars lined up trying to get out.

Thick vines had woven themselves into the bars of the gate and essentially locked the residents inside. The owners of the cars were pulling the vines down and one man had pulled a machete from his trunk and was furiously hacking at a particularly knotty one.

And there was Timothy.

Hanging upside down on the fence, his foot caught in a tangle of vines. He was yelling at the people for help, but they were trying too hard to *get out*. They weren't about to stop in order to help some idiot *get in*.

Timothy saw Leah and Effie coming toward him.

"Leah! Leah!"

She climbed onto the gate and pulled on the vines until she freed his foot. He fell to the concrete and picked himself up and looked around.

"What's burning?" he said.

"The whole world, I think," Leah said.

"I was trying to get here as fast as I could. I wanted to help you."

"I know."

"I guess I'm not gonna be much help."

Effie and says, "Big hero. Sir Gawain, couldn't even get in the door."

The three of them sat on the grass and watched the others clear the gate and pry it open. By then the panic had subsided. The fire had stopped at the wall, and other than some scorched St. Augustine, the Greymont was undamaged.

Timothy leaned over and whispered in Leah's ear, "I'm here to stay. If you want me."

She pulled him to her and kissed him as if tomorrow had been cancelled. They lay on the grass and soon were breathing hard.

Effie said, "For pity's sake. Not out here in public. Let's go back to the apartment. I have to pee."

EPILOGUE

What are roots that clutch, what branches grow
out of this stony rubbish? Son of man you cannot
say or guess....
~T. S. Eliot

Leah stretched like a cat in the king-sized bed. They were staying in the Four Seasons Resort on the big island in Hawaii. Timothy was in the shower, singing at the tops of his lungs.

Ed Sheerin? she thought. *My god. What have you signed on for, girl?*

She and Timothy had taken Effie to a luau last night. They had eaten roasted pig and drunk pineapple drinks like real tourists. Effie enjoyed herself, but tired out early. After they got her to her suite and into bed, they took a long walk on the beach. The moon stood on the horizon and frosted the tops of the waves with white light. Leah stopped, kicked off her sandals, and stepped into the warm water.

"Come here and kiss me," she said.

He obliged her.

She put her hands under his garish silk shirt and traced her fingers across the muscles of his back.

"You may need to run me back to the hotel and, I don't know, sex me up, Gawain."

"I'm not sure," he said. "I have a lot of pig in me I need to walk off before I'm ready for bed."

"You got that right, Porky."

She was teasing him, of course.

You could bounce a Krugerrand off his abs.

"But you promised that if I let you come along with me, you'd make me see God."

"Well," he said. "A promise is a promise."

Their lovemaking was revelatory, epiphanic, Biblical even, for she saw God three times before he came up for air. His body was rock hard, like a carving or a petrograph. Like a stone icon from a temple in a lost city in the tropical jungle. She didn't mean to, but she climaxed again when he did. They lay back, bathed in sweat and moonlight.

"I'm glad I brought you along," she said and giggled.

"What are you talking about, Leah. I bought the tickets, booked the suites..."

His brother, Edward, Little Eddie, had finally screwed things up so badly at work that Timothy's father had reinstated him, released his trust fund so he was rich again, and told him he could work from Tennessee or anywhere else he wanted if he would just go straighten out the Madrid office once and for all.

It had taken Timothy a month in Spain.

Leah had spent the time planning her Hawaii trip.

"No, no, no, rich boy. I was coming here anyway. All you did was upgrade the trip to first class."

He sighed.

"Fine. I'm glad you brought me too."

They fell asleep in each other's arms.

And now Timothy was emerging from the shower. She knew she should probably take one now too. But the sight of his body!

Lord a mercy, she thought.

So, she got out of the bed and stood by the window naked. She stretched her arms and shook out her long red hair. In a quick minute he predictably pulled her to the bed and began kissing her breasts and was very quickly inside her. When she came, she slipped out from under him and left him, still hard, on the wrinkled sheets.

"Hold that thought for me," she said. "I'm coming back for it later."

God, you're a tease! She thought.

After the woods behind her apartment burned, Timothy had moved to Knoxville. He rented a house on the east side of town, about three miles from the Greymont. He set about winning her heart, which he did by winning Effie's.

He came over and cooked three or four nights a week. He was teaching himself to cook, and between Effie's lessons and the internet, he was making tremendous progress. Timothy also hung out with Effie most days while Leah was at the university, teaching and trying to make inroads into the politics of the department. He also took Effie out—to the mall, the park, a senior center where they both played bingo, Timothy working both their cards and talking a blue streak to her. He charmed the Oklahoma bloomers off her.

Eventually, he talked Leah into moving in with him. They spent several Saturdays and Sundays hauling Effie around to open houses until each of them was satisfied with one, and he bought it. The house was huge, more room than they needed. *Rich boy!* And of course, it was in a ritzy neighborhood. Red brick with white columns on the front, its angular construction softened the Colonial look she didn't care for.

Who are you kidding? The place is a palace.

And more good news. Instead of being repelled by Leah's misuse of her grant money at Yale, her department chair and the senior faculty at Tennessee thought it was hilarious and urged her to continue her studies in evil places. They suggested that the publication of such a book (with a reputable academic publisher, of course) would be a giant step toward tenure. She began planning a summer trip.

She had been reading about Mauna Loa. A two-and-a-half-mile tall volcano, with a lava field of eight hundred square kilometers, it was the biggest volcano in the world. More to the point, local legends say that it is home to the Hawaiian goddess of fire, Madame Pele. Leah liked the idea, a female god of fire.

On her walks through the Whittington Creek neighborhood, she considered the various possibilities. Hawaii would be an expensive trip. She would have to take Effie. She wasn't sure if Timothy would be able to come. He still had to go to Spain for his father. She was sure he would want to, but she wasn't going to pressure him. He'd just reconciled with his father, and she didn't want to sour that. It would be much cheaper just to visit the Smoking Ghost Town up in Centralia, Pennsylvania. They could drive that together.

But during her walks, off in the distance, she kept seeing a woman in a flowing red dress walking a little white dog. Something about her intrigued Leah, and she tried on several occasions to catch up with her, to talk to her, but she never could.

What? Are you going to ask her whether to go to Hawaii or Pennsylvania?

Then one day, she found a website that went into more detail about Madame Pele. "Rumblings in Mauna Loa are said to herald her emergence to warn people of coming eruptions. Reports of sightings of Madame Pele span two hundred years. She shows up on forest roads or in other public places. Although her age varies, she is always wearing a red muumuu and is usually accompanied by a small white dog."

Really?

That was that. Hawaii or bust. She'd just wait till he got back from Spain.

Timothy had rented a jeep, and they loaded Effie up after breakfast and headed for Mauna Loa. The lava field stretched out before them like a black nightmare wasteland. They left Effie at the Visitors Center with some other older folks who had no interest in trekking a lava field and took off on foot. Timothy kept asking whether or not the volcano might erupt while they were stuck out in the middle of a flow. He kept looking askance at the peak of the mountain. For some reason, she liked him nervous and watchful.

"Maybe," she said.

There was something in the pattern of the flow. The waves, the swirls, the sweeping crags and points frozen like black ice.

There was something to be read here, deciphered. She found an indentation where the swirls looked like runes. Almost like something she could read. At the bottom, between two frozen waves of black lava, a tiny green tendril and leaf protruded from cold black rock. Green life in all this black death. There was something very familiar about it.

About the Author

John Calvin Hughes

John Calvin Hughes has published in numerous magazines and journals, including *Dead Mule*, *Southern Indiana Review*, *Autumn Sky Poetry*, *The Timberline Review*, *The American Journal of Poetry*, and *Mississippi Review*. His publications include a critical study, *The Novels and Short Stories of Frederick Barthelme* (The Edwin Mellen Press); two poetry chapbooks, *The Shape of Our Luck* (Sargent Press) and *Cul-de-sac Agonistes* (Black Bomb Books); a full-length poetry collection, *Music from a Farther Room* (Aldrich Press); and four novels, *Twilight of the Lesser Gods* (CreateSpace), *Killing Rush* (Second Wind Publishing), *The Lost Gospel of Darnell Rabren* (Bowen Press Books), and *The Boys* (Regal House). Nominated for a Pushcart in 2015, he is also the winner of the Ilse and Hans Juergensen Poetry Contest and The Thomas Burnett Swann Poetry Prize. He lives and works in Florida.